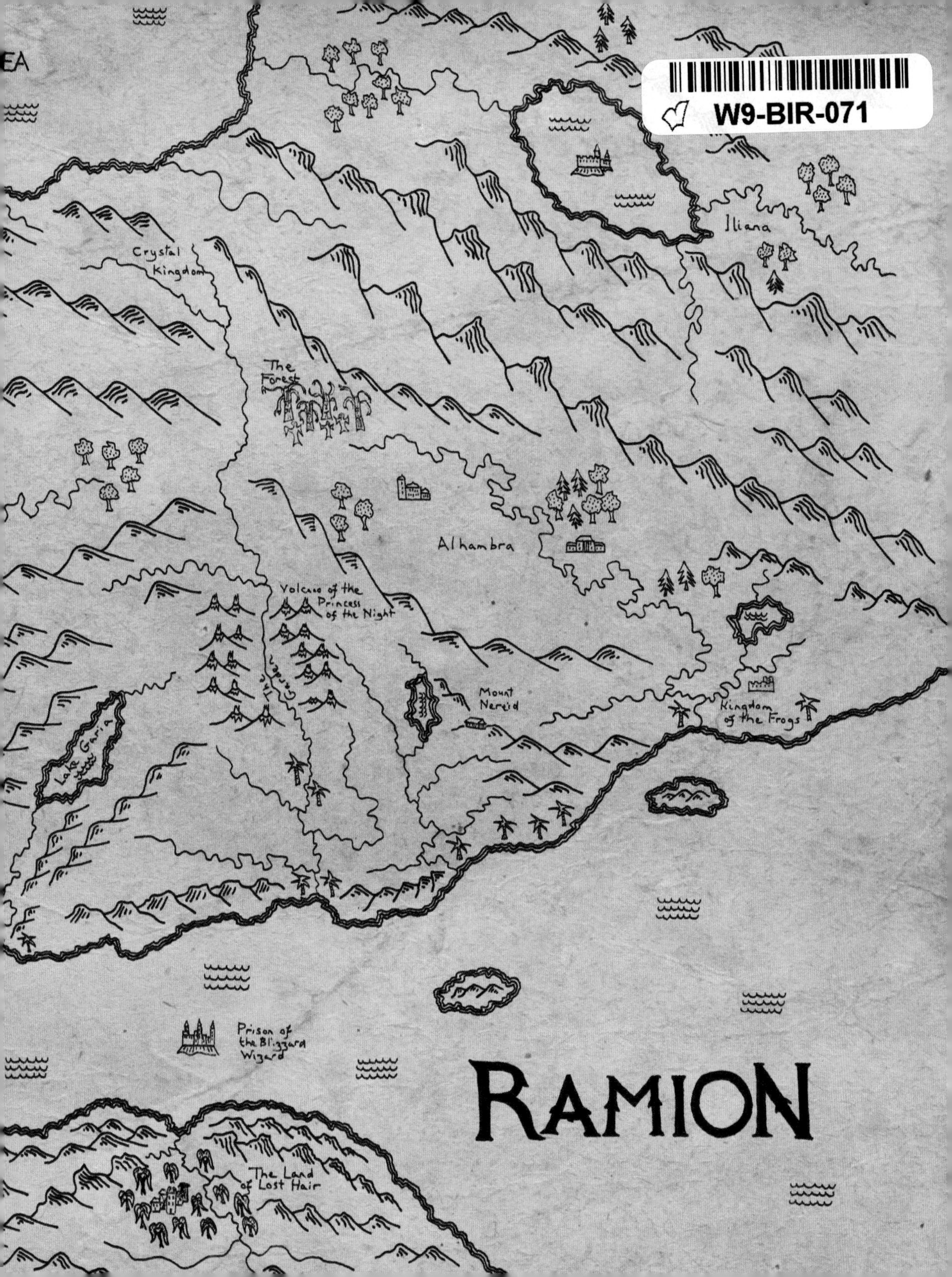
Crystal Kingdom
Iliana
The Forest
Alhambra
Volcano of the Princess of the Night
Lake Garia
Mount Nereid
Kingdom of the Frogs
Prison of the Blizzard Wizard
RAMION
The Land of Lost Hair

THE DREAM THIEF

Published by
Perronet Press
www.ramion-books.com
Copyright © Text and illustrations
Frank Hinks 2018

A CIP record for this book is available from the British Library

ISBN: 9781909938021

Printed in China by CP Printing Ltd.
Layout by Jennifer Stephens

TALES OF RAMION
THE DREAM THIEF

FRANK HINKS

Perronet
2018

TALES OF RAMION

THE GARDENER

Lord of Ramion, guardian and protector

SNUGGLE

Dream Lord sent to protect the boys from the witch Griselda

JULIUS
ALEXANDER
BENJAMIN

Three brothers who long for adventure

SCROOEY-LOOEY

Greedy, rude, half-mad rabbit, a friend of the boys

SUSAN

The boys' mother as a child

LITTLE DREAM

A dream of destiny, a friend for Ben

PRECIOUS DREAM PLANT

Has the power to reverse evil magic

GRISELDA THE GRUNCH

A witch who longs to eat the boys

THE DIM DAFT DWARVES

Julioso, Aliano, Benjio, Griselda's guards

BORIS

Griselda's pet skull, strangely fond of her

NIGHTMARE CHILD

Burps crimson blood

PRINCESS
OF THE NIGHT

*Lord of Nothingness,
source of evil*

GNARGS

*Warrior servants of
the Princess*

THE DREAM THIEF

*Sucks up dreams,
keeps them in his belly*

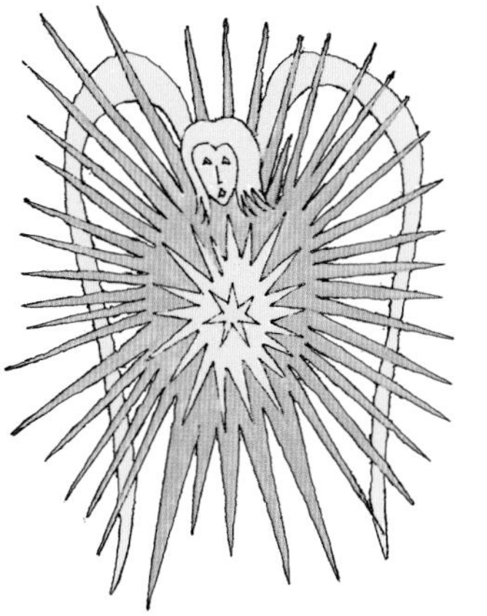

Chapter One

The boys were supposed to be asleep, but were talking quietly in Julius's bedroom when Snuggle hurried to them. "We must save your mother's dream," he said. The boys looked at the cat in blank amazement. Children have time for dreams, but surely not mothers – they are too busy. "Of course mothers have dreams," responded the cat, reading their thoughts. "Get dressed. Join hands. Think of the Land of Ramion."

The boys got dressed, joined hands and as Snuggle breathed upon them they travelled through the void to the hillside above the Garden in the Land of Ramion. The Guide was waiting for them. He led them down the gully to the Garden, then through the Garden. The Garden was bathed in a strange silver light, but whether the light radiated from the moon and shooting stars or from the Gardener the boys could not tell.

The Gardener was waiting for them near a bonfire beside the lake. He was wearing robes of blue and silver and a cloak of gold. Around his body glowed an aura of majesty and power. The boys looked at him in awe.

"Welcome! Welcome!" cried the Gardener smiling. "It is the Night of Dreams. Your mother is in danger of losing her dream. Come sit beside me."

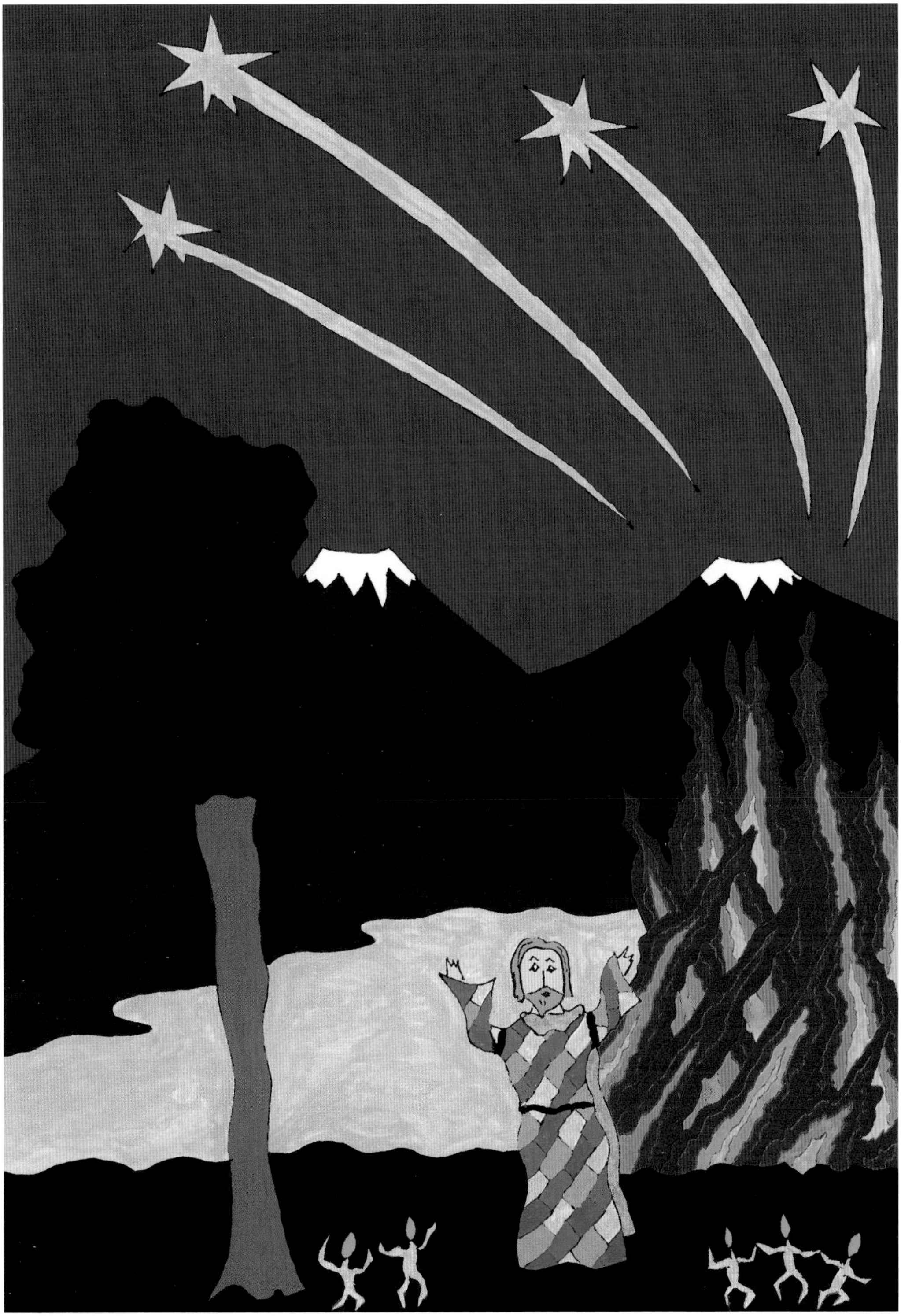

The boys, Snuggle and the Gardener sat on the ground beside the fire. Embers flew up into the night sky, each spark a dream. Some faded and died. But every now and then an ember turned into a shooting star which blazed silver across the night sky. As the boys sat around the fire the Gardener told them about the Night of Dreams. "Dreams of Destiny are like a guiding star. Follow that star and you will achieve what you were born to do, you will fulfil your destiny. On the Night of Dreams boys and girls, men and women discover their special dream or dreams, discover what they were born to do. Boys: look into the fire. What can you see?"

Julius looked into the fire long and hard, and deep amongst the flames he saw letters of the alphabet rising up, coming together, forming words that tumbled and jumped and linked together forming patterns, one after another. "I can see letters and words and sentences," he cried. "I am going to be a writer."

Alexander looked intently into the fire. He was completely still until suddenly he cried, "I can see colours merging together, making images on a canvas. I am going to be an artist," he said firmly, adding after a pause, "Like Mum."

Benjamin stared and stared deep into the fire, and disappointed cried, "I can see nothing but flame. Is there no special dream for me?" he asked the Gardener.

"There is. But you must find it."

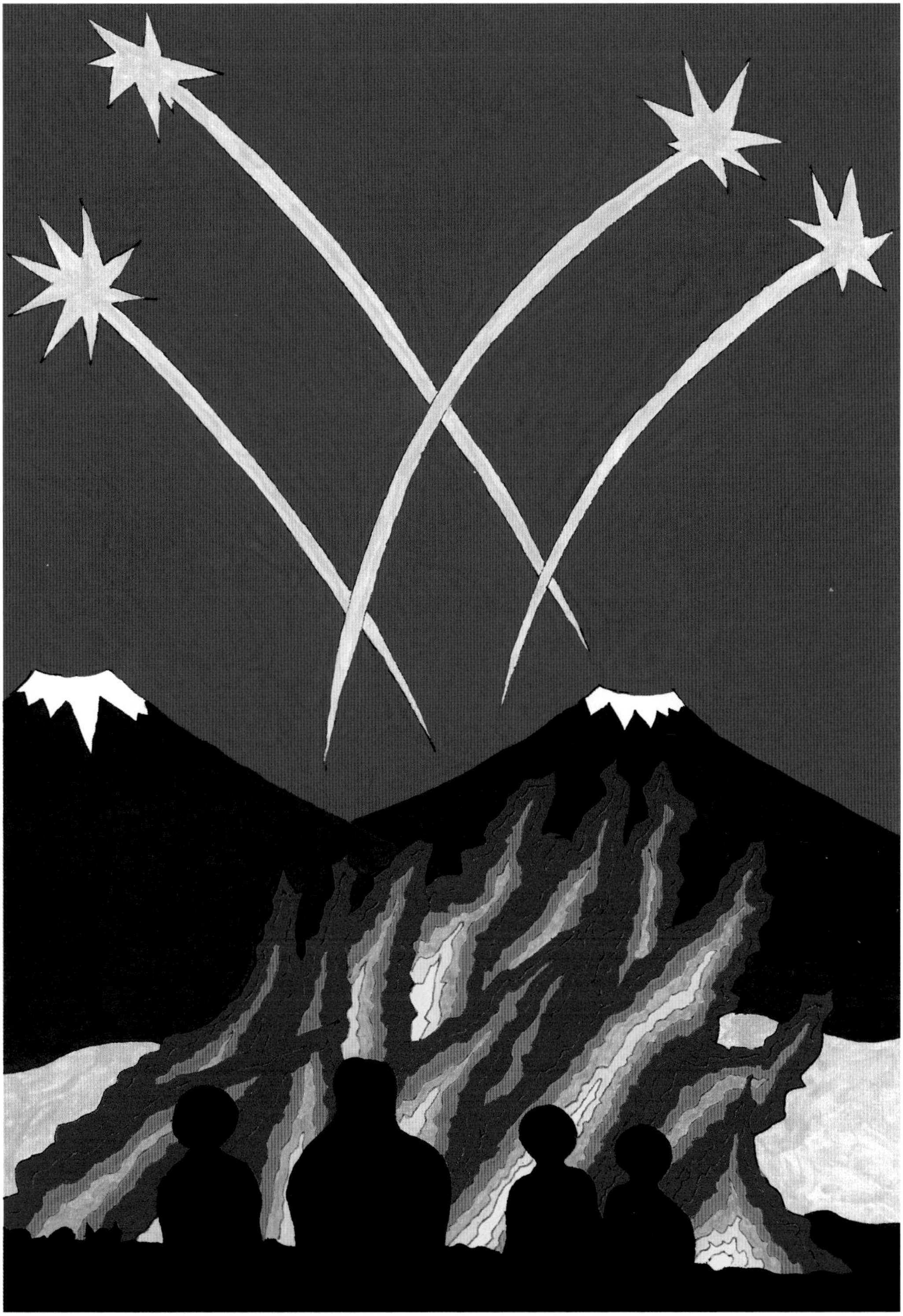

"But what about our Mum?" asked Julius. "Snuggle said we have to save her dream."

"You do," the Gardener replied. "On the Night of Dreams people not only gain dreams. They lose them." "But how?" "Dreams of Destiny (when they come to a boy or girl) want to become real, to become realised, as some describe it. But people neglect their dreams, do nothing to make them real. On the Night of Dreams a dream may decide to leave such a person, to return to the Land of Dreams."

"Is that about to happen to Mum?"

"No. The danger to your mother and her dream is far far worse. If a dream returns to the Land of Dreams it continues to live. It can become the dream of a different person. It can even return to the person from whom it fled. But if a dream is stolen by the Dream Thief the dream becomes a dried up husk and the person loses the dream for ever."

"Poor dream!" "Poor Mum!" "Poor both of them!" cried the boys.

"But look into the fire." Looking deep into the fire the boys saw their mother asleep back home in The Old Vicarage. She was surrounded by her dreams, busy, bright, colourful dreams of the boys, choirs and music festival, but the dream of being an artist was beginning to fade, to turn grey as music swirled around it. The dream was not happy.

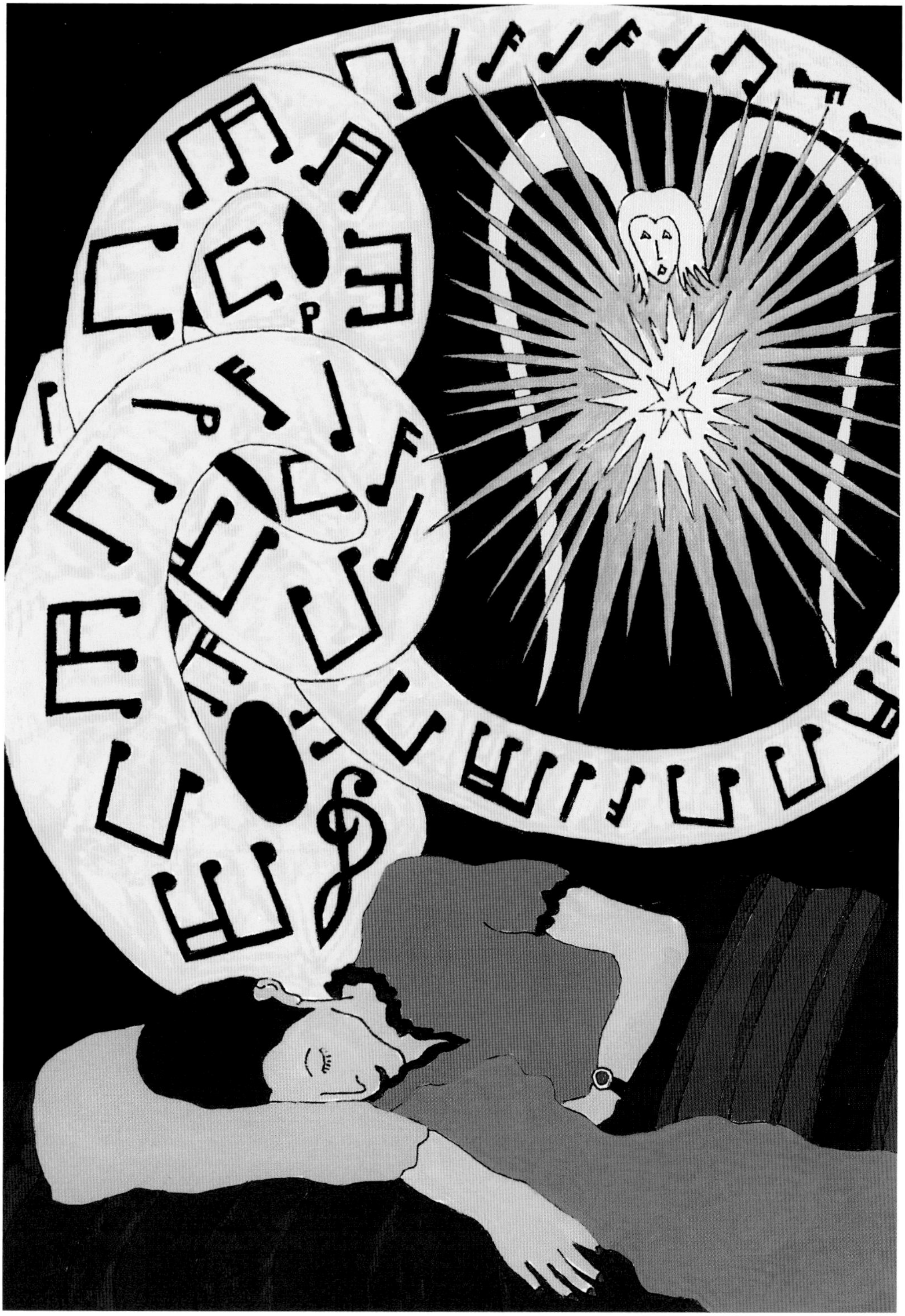

"What is the matter?" asked the boys. "Your mother's dream of being an artist is starting to fade," the Gardener replied. "As it weakens the Dream Thief will get the chance to steal it."

"But does that matter? She has us." "She has her choirs and music festival – even though we think they are boring." "She has The Old Vicarage – even Dad, though she is not very keen on his dancing."

"They are not enough. She was born with the dream of becoming an artist, a painter, a sculptor. If she loses that dream, she will never be happy."

At that moment volcanoes around the Garden erupted, spitting fire into the night sky. Ash passed across the face of the moon. When the boys looked back into the fire they saw a revolting creature with head of a bird, tongue of an anteater and great fat bouncing belly creep away leading their mother's dream of being an artist by the hand. "The dream!" "The dream!" "What is happening to it?"

"The Dream Thief has stolen it. Rescue your mother's dream. Snuggle will help you. Whatever happens in the Land of Dreams keep travelling. Never give up." At that Snuggle took Alex and Benje by the hand. Alex reached out to Julius. The Gardener raised his hand in blessing as the cat breathed on the boys. Protected by the magic breath cat and boys dived deep into the fire, down and down through flame, down towards the Land of Dreams.

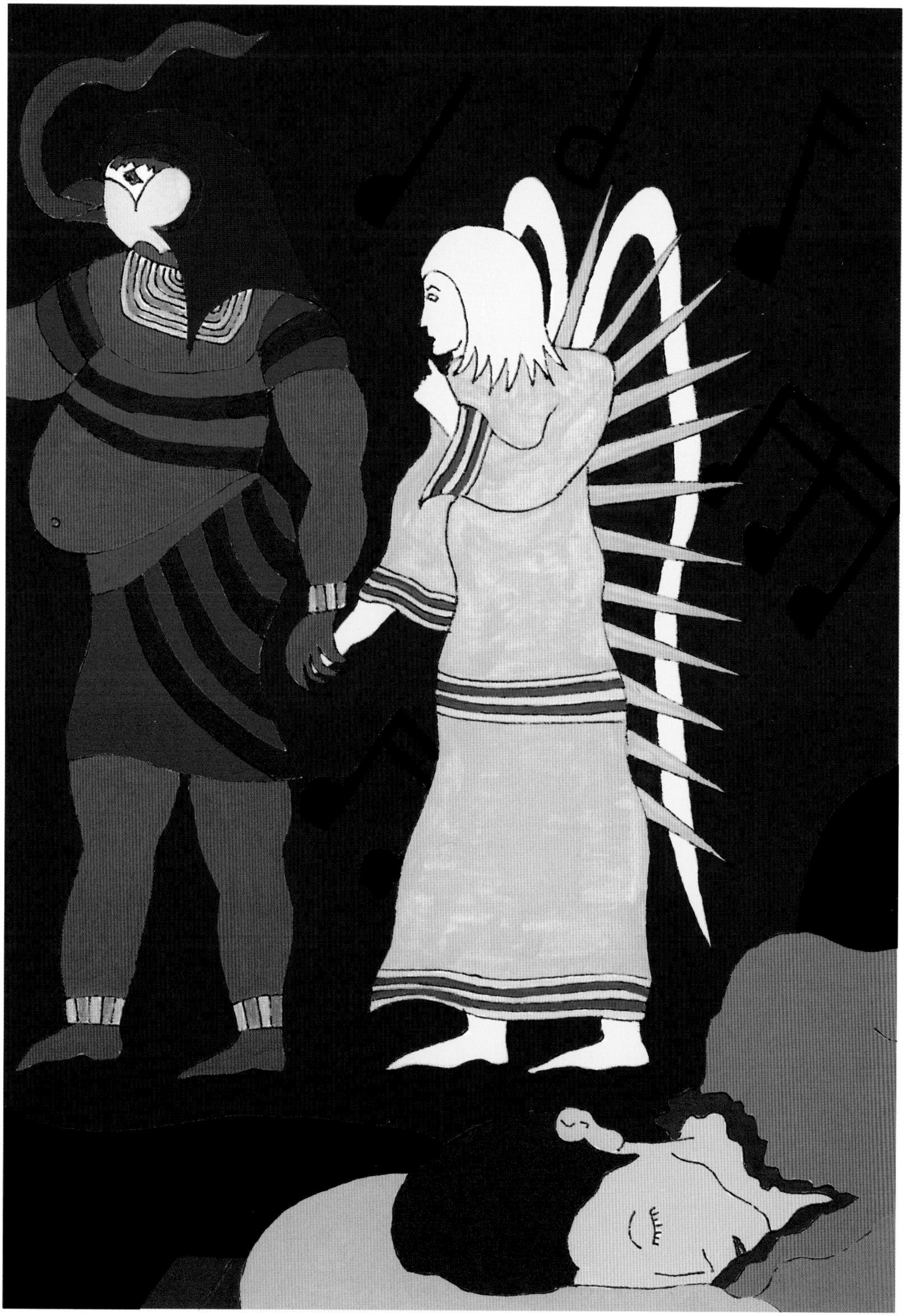

Chapter Two

The entrance to the Land of Dreams was not what Snuggle expected. For thousands of years two gates led to and from the dream realm, one fashioned of sawn ivory through which false dreams passed to deceive people, the other of polished horn through which truthful, prophetic dreams winged their way. Recently the gates of ivory and horn had been blocked and replaced by departure and arrival halls based on Toronto airport.

No dream knew how this change had come about. The dreams were used to passing to and from the dream realm free of control when suddenly they learnt that the Land of Dreams had joined the Inter-Galactic Treaty on Movement Control and had recruited Immigration Officers from the planet Zak (who had very small brains and pointy heads). The Immigration Officers when appointed were shocked at the way dreams came and went free of control. They looked through the universe for a system which would cause the dreams as much inconvenience as possible. By happy chance they alighted upon the practices of Canadian Immigration.

The Arrivals Hall was vast. Thousands and thousands of dreams (of all colours, shapes and sizes) were queuing to get back into the Land of Dreams. Though unaccustomed to queuing most dreams queued patiently, but not the Nightmares who as usual were making trouble.

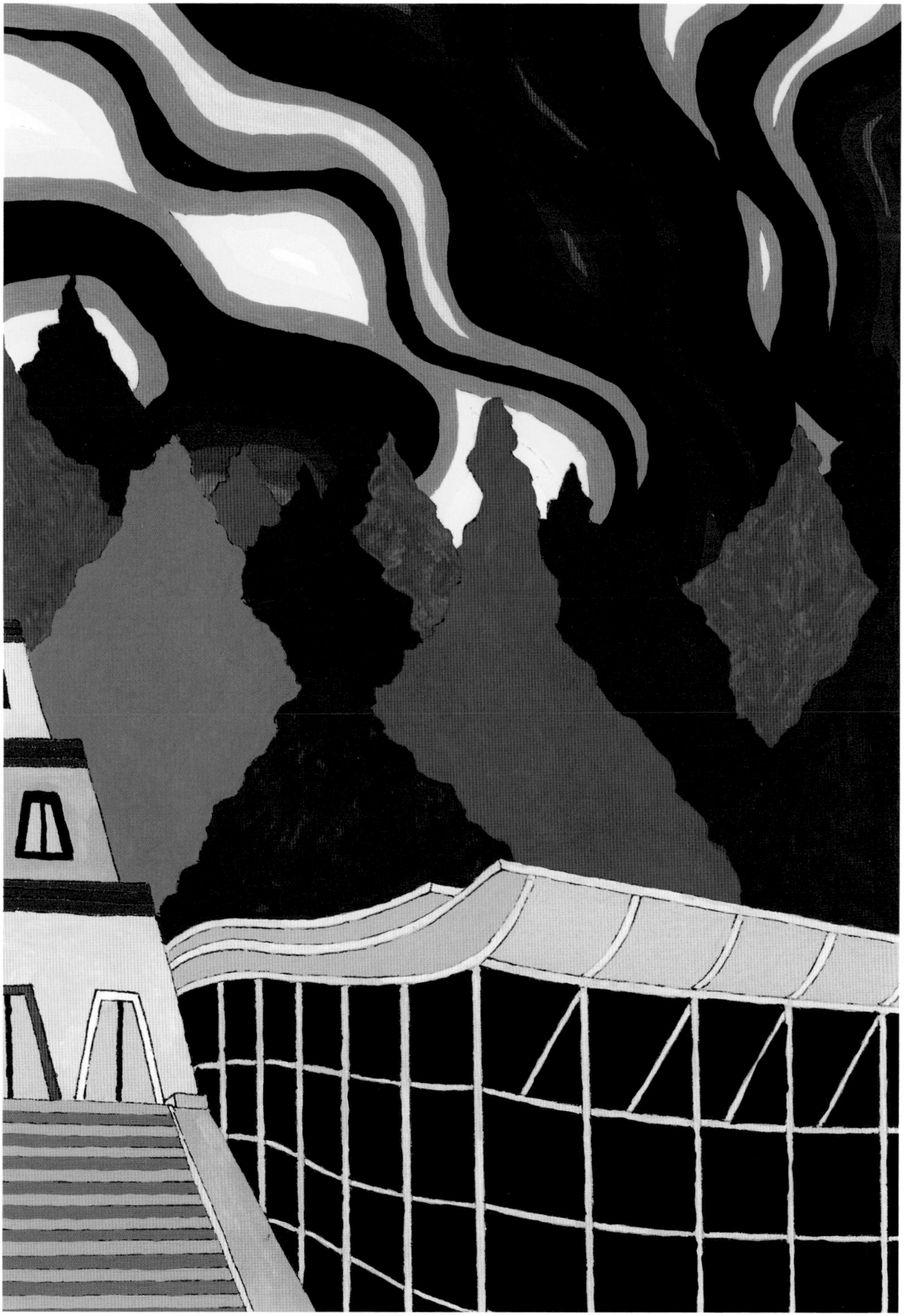

Nightmares of Gothic black (like aged rock stars) crept up on poor little Day Dreams, and made them scream. Others put on shows of blood and gore causing dreams of a more sensitive disposition to faint.

At the head of the queue was a line of desks and cubicles. Since it was the Night of Dreams (a night when far more dreams returned to the dream world than usual) most of the cubicles (like Toronto at the end of a public holiday) were closed. But in a few sat Immigration Officers with rubber stamps and multi-coloured felt tip pens, making unnecessary conversation, dealing with each arrival as slowly as possible. Beyond them were the entrances to the Land of Dreams, no longer made of ivory or horn but of steel with plastic nameplates explaining who was to pass through each entrance: (1) Daydreams; (2) False dreams; (3) True dreams; (4) Dreams of Destiny; (5) Nightmares; (6) Aliens; and (7) Immigration Officers (from other lands) and other VIPs ("Very Important Persons," explained Julius to his brothers).

The boys and cat queued patiently for hours. Benje wanted to play with Nightmare Child (a child of seething shades of green and purple who let out burps of crimson blood) but his brothers told him not to be so stupid.

At last they reached the head of the queue.

"Stay behind the yellow line," said Snuggle. "I'll go first."

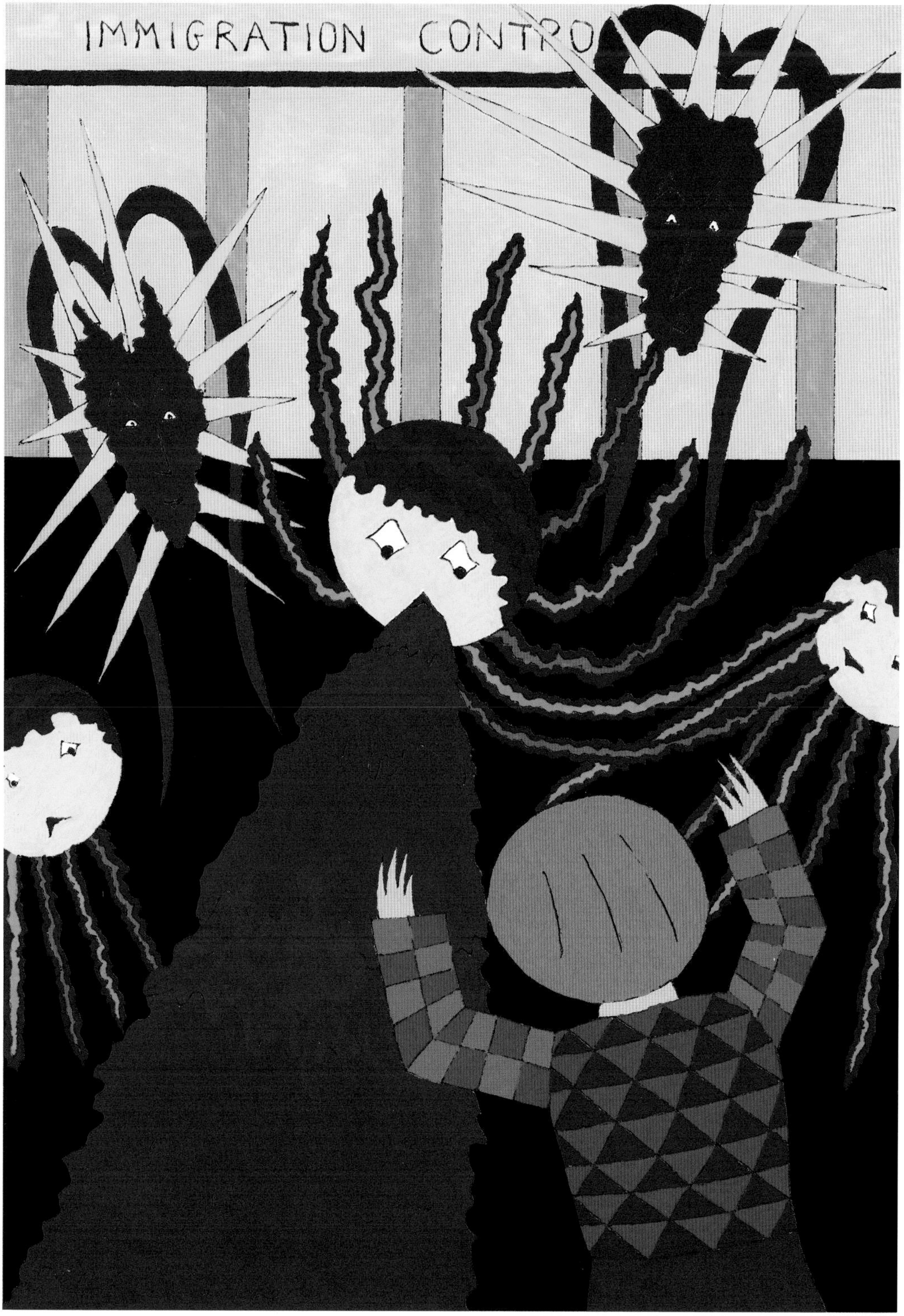
IMMIGRATION CONTRO

As Snuggle approached the cubicle the Immigration Officer rose to his feet, bowed low and murmured, "We are honoured to be visited by a Dream Lord. There is no need for me to check your papers. Go through the exit for VIPs."

"I'll wait for you on the other side," called out Snuggle to the boys. The rules were very strict: having gone through immigration Snuggle had to depart by the exit for VIPs.

The boys did not get on so well. They were not Dream Lords, they were not guardians of the realm of dreams: they were mere mortals. The Immigration Officer looked at the boys with deep suspicion. He handled their papers with evident disgust, and asked, "What is the purpose of your visit? Holiday or business?"

"Business," replied Julius firmly. "We are looking for our mother's dream."

The Immigration Officer snorted. "It is for the Custody Officers of the Land of Dreams to look for dreams which have gone missing. We cannot have mere mortals taking their jobs." With three flourishes of the pen he put pink lines through the papers of the boys. "Go up the stairs to Immigration Control. Stop wasting my time. Off you go." He rubbed his hands in glee. Like Nightmares Immigration Officers really enjoy their work.

With heavy hearts the boys walked past the Immigration Officer towards the stairs. As they passed the VIP exit Snuggle (who was waiting just inside) called out, "I'll wait for you."

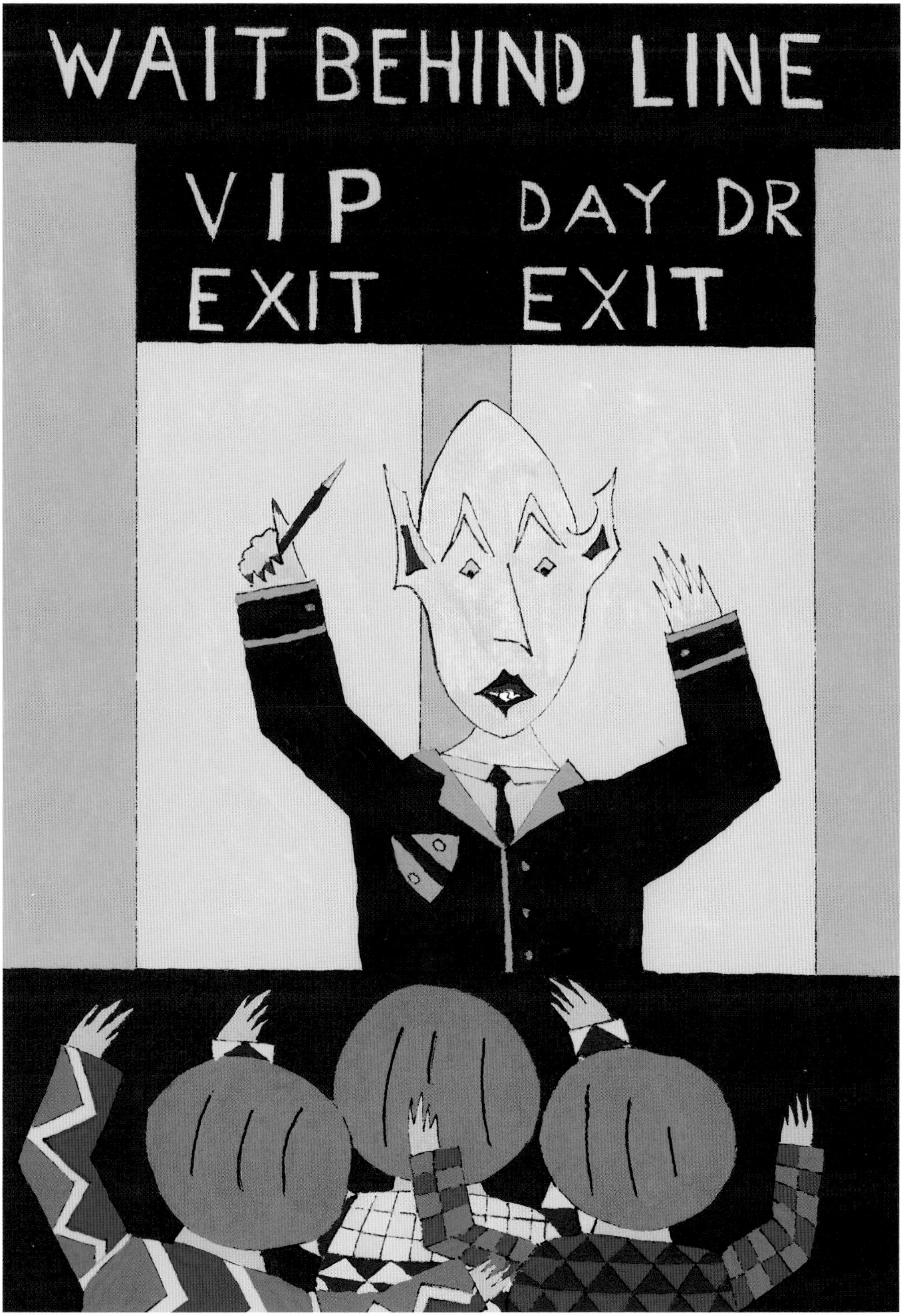
WAIT BEHIND LINE
VIP EXIT
DAY DR EXIT

When Benjamin heard the cat he burst into tears (for he was only little) and called out, "Snuggle! Snuggle! I'm coming to you."

As Benjamin darted towards the VIP exit two burly Enforcement Officers blocked the way. They looked much like Nightmares, but without their sense of humour: one touch of their arms and the mind of a boy (or girl) will fill with terror.

"I want to see my cat," cried Benjamin, tears giving way to anger. "Get out of the way."

"Desist! Desist!" commanded one Enforcement Officer. "Before we fill your mind with terror!" added the other.

Julius and Alexander darted forward, took their brother by the arms, and led him protesting up the stairs. Immigration Control was not so large as the Arrivals Hall, but full of hundreds of unhappy dreams queuing gloomily. They were the flotsam and jetsam of the realm of dreams, the dregs of dream world. There were Day Dreams who had been partying and lost their papers. There were would-be football stars and celebrities, Dreams of Destiny not noted for their brains who had filled in their papers incorrectly. There were no Nightmares: the Immigration Officers were too frightened to refuse them admission. The boys were the only Aliens.

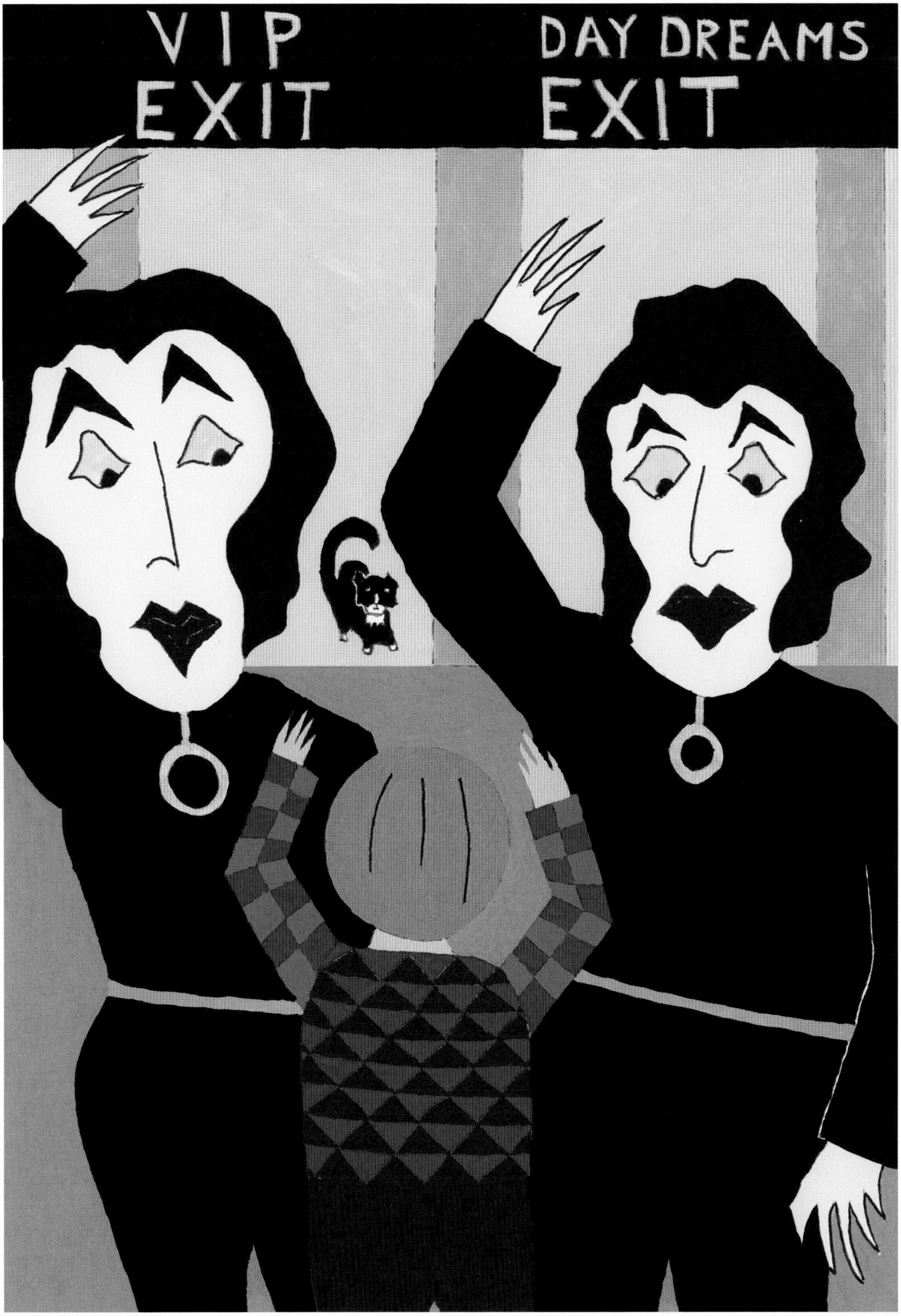
VIP
EXIT
DAY DREAMS
EXIT

The boys queued for hours until they reached the front of the queue. Before they could approach the window with "Chief Immigration Officer" inscribed in gold two lesser Immigration Officers came up to them and demanded to see their papers. "You are Aliens. You should not be queuing here."

"But we have queued for hours!" protested the boys.

"No cheek from you!" replied one Immigration Officer. "Not unless you want to start queuing again in the Arrivals Hall," added the other.

"Then tell us what we should do," said the boys wearily.

The Immigration Officers conferred amongst themselves. Like all Immigration Officers they did nothing fast. Eventually one said, "It is thousands of years since a mortal last visited the Land of Dreams. Now four in one day. Join the other Alien in Room 533 whilst we decide what to do with you."

"Do with us!" "I don't like the sound of that!" "Nor me!" whispered the boys.

But they had no choice. They followed the Immigration Officers to Room 533 where a little girl was waiting. She was not happy.

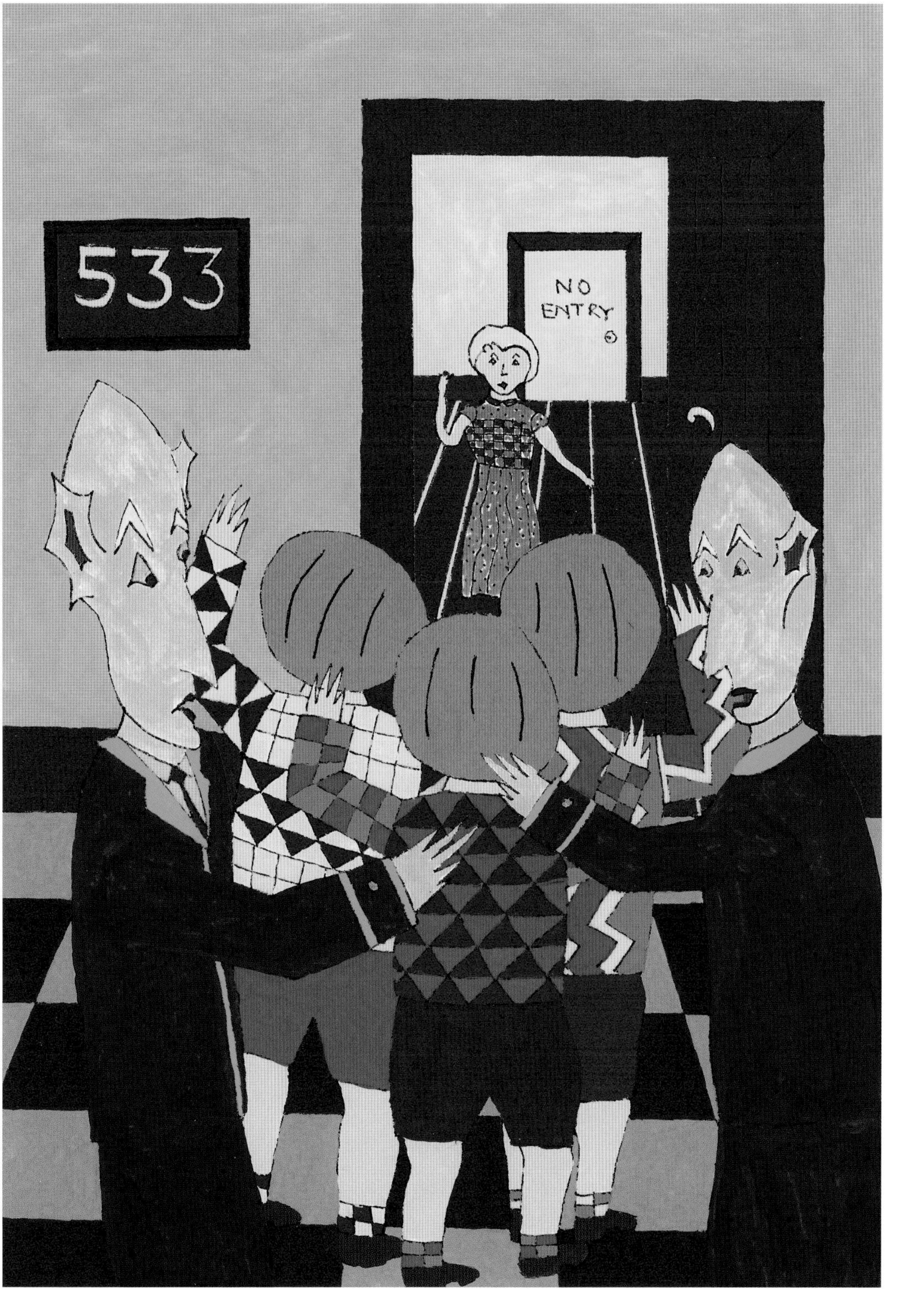
533
NO ENTRY

CHAPTER THREE

"Hi! I'm Julius. These are my brothers Alex and Benje. What is your name?" "Susan," replied the girl, wiping tears from her eyes. "I have lost my dream. One moment I was drawing happily with my crayons, dreaming of becoming an artist. The next moment my dream had gone. Then I found myself here."

Alex whispered to his brothers, "It's Mum! I've seen a picture of her when young up in the cottage attic." "Don't tell her we are her sons," replied Julius, "The knowledge would freak her out." "And if she finds out what Ben is like she might decide she doesn't want children and we might never exist!" added Alex. At this (not surprisingly) Benjamin kicked Alexander and they fell fighting to the ground.

"Stop fighting, boys!" commanded the little girl in an amazingly loud voice.

The boys stopped fighting, "Wow!" they cried. "What a voice!" "Just like Mum!" "If we are not careful she will stand us in the corner!"

"I am here to find my dream. Why are you here?" asked the little girl.

"We have come to help you find your dream," the boys replied.

"Why?"

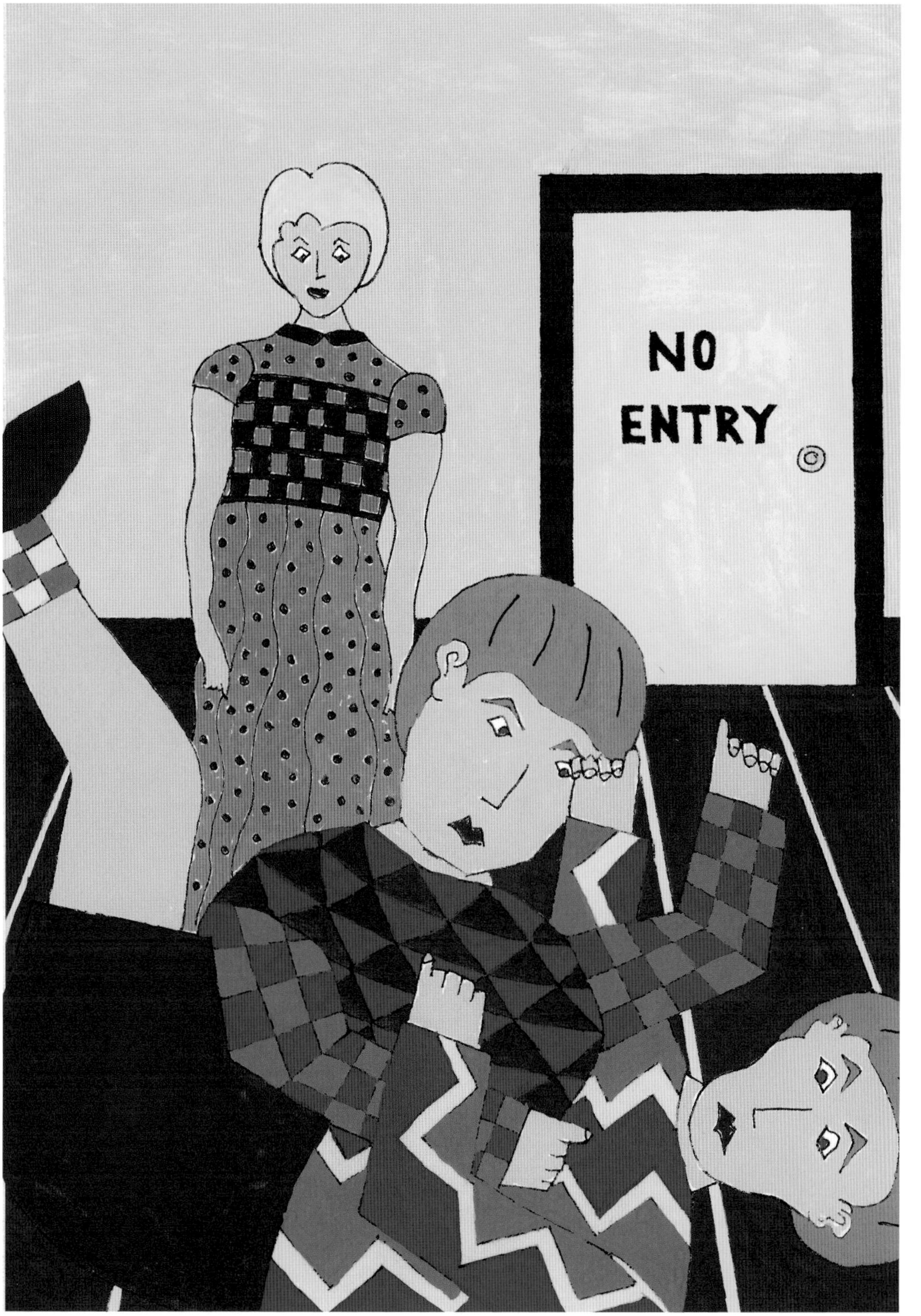
NO
ENTRY

Julius thought fast. How could he explain why they had come without revealing that they were her children. At last he said, "Our cat Snuggle is a Dream Lord, a guardian of dreams. He told us that we must come and help you." To Susan this sounded entirely reasonable. She also had a cat, not a Dream Lord, but to her very special.

Then they heard shouting in the corridor. Alex rushed to the door. He looked cautiously outside. Trembling with fear he closed the door quietly and turned to his brothers. "It's the Princess of the Night and a revolting creature with huge fat belly and long pointy tongue."

"Who is the Princess of the Night?" asked Susan.

"Not someone you would like to meet. If she gets half a chance she will turn you into a statue and add you to her art collection." Susan agreed that this was not something to be desired.

Then Julius said, "We must get out of here," for he had just noticed a door at the back of Room 533. Swiftly he opened the door, then screamed, "Not such a good idea!!!" as he and his brothers and Susan were sucked into a tunnel and spat out into the Place of Nightmares.

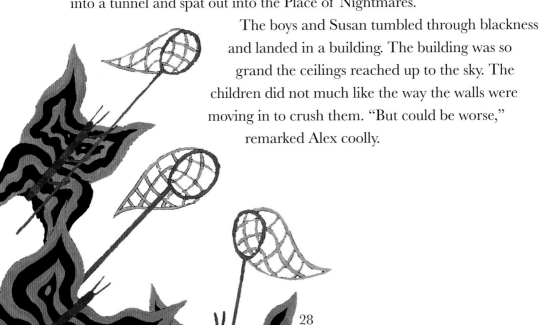

The boys and Susan tumbled through blackness and landed in a building. The building was so grand the ceilings reached up to the sky. The children did not much like the way the walls were moving in to crush them. "But could be worse," remarked Alex coolly.

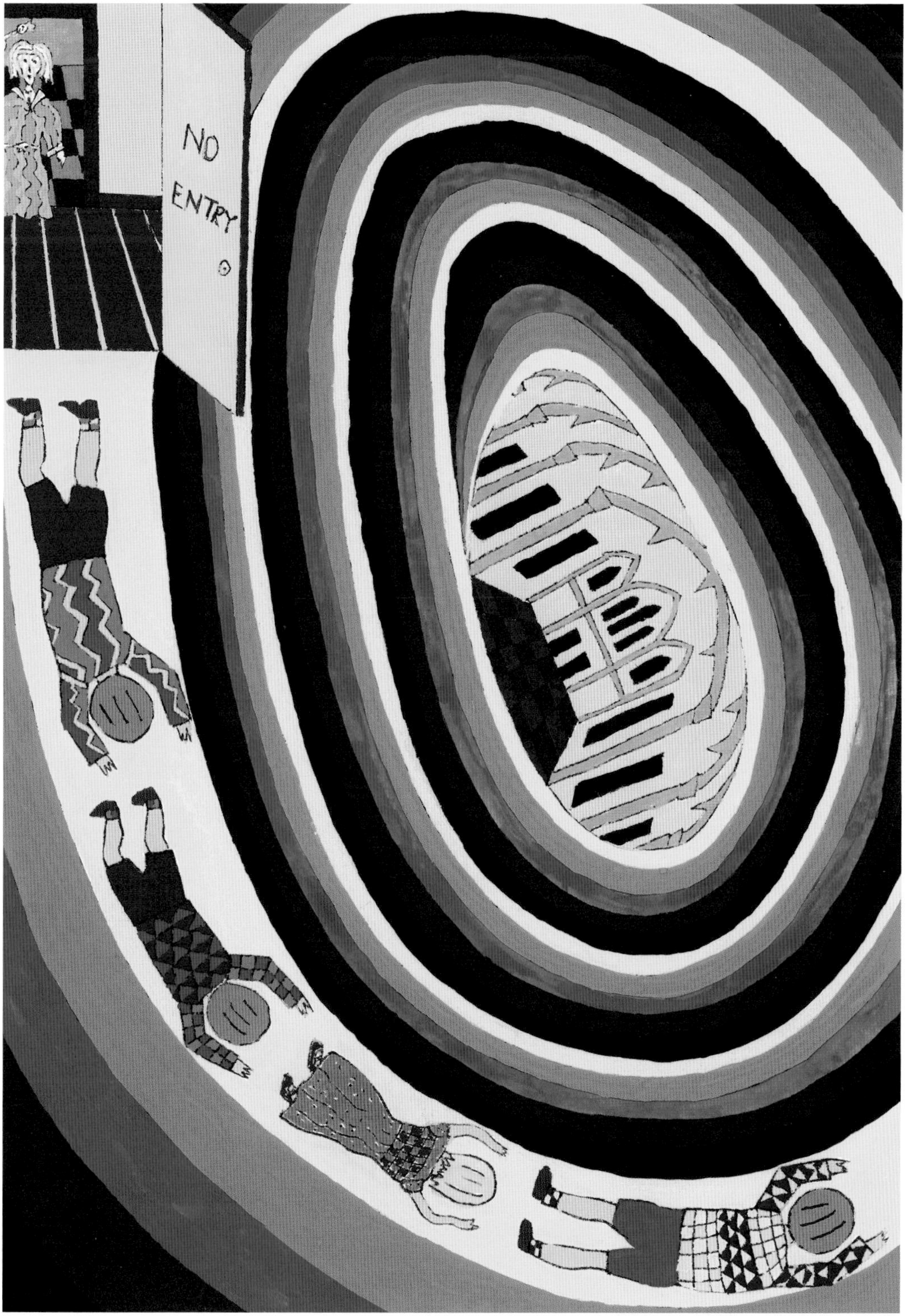
NO
ENTRY

Then great monster heads started to emerge from the walls. With winking eyes and leering mouths their tongues shot out trying to sweep the boys and girl into their gaping mouths.

"Not so good," gasped Julius as he and Alexander took Susan and Benje by the hand and began to run. Then the building burst into flame.

"Help! Help! Help!" cried Benjamin and Susan as fires blazed around them.

Then a wall collapsed. An opening appeared. "Through the gap!" shouted Julius leading the way.

The boys and girl found themselves in a raging violet sky. They were standing on a narrow edge of stone. Each side plummeted down thousands of feet. In the middle of an electric storm they fell to their knees, hugged the ground in terror as lightning and thunder flashed and crashed around them and howling winds tried to tear them from the edge. It was not pleasant, not pleasant at all.

Then the boys and Susan became aware that they were not alone on the edge. A cat was with them. "Snuggle!" "Help!" "I'm losing my grip!"

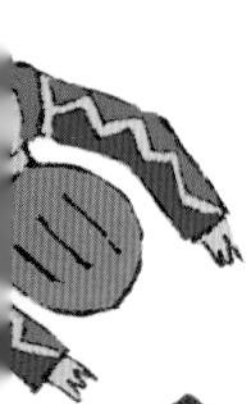

"In the Place of Nightmares there is nothing to fear but fear itself," replied the cat. "Join hands." Boys and girl joined hands. "Now jump off the edge."

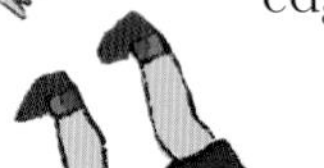

"I can't! I can't!" screamed Susan unaware of Snuggle's magic powers.

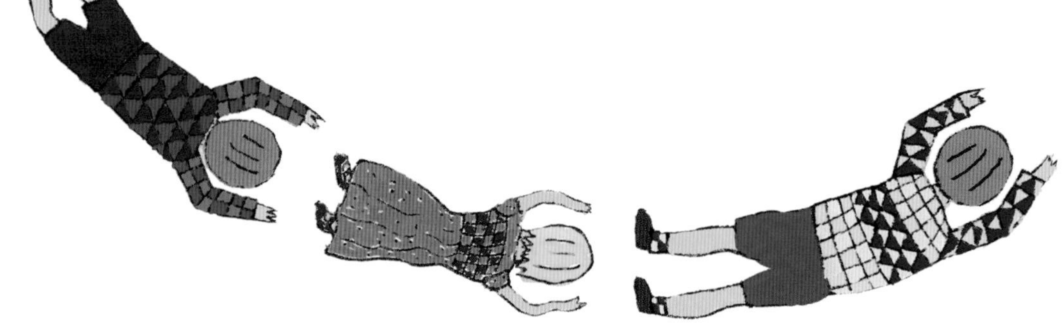

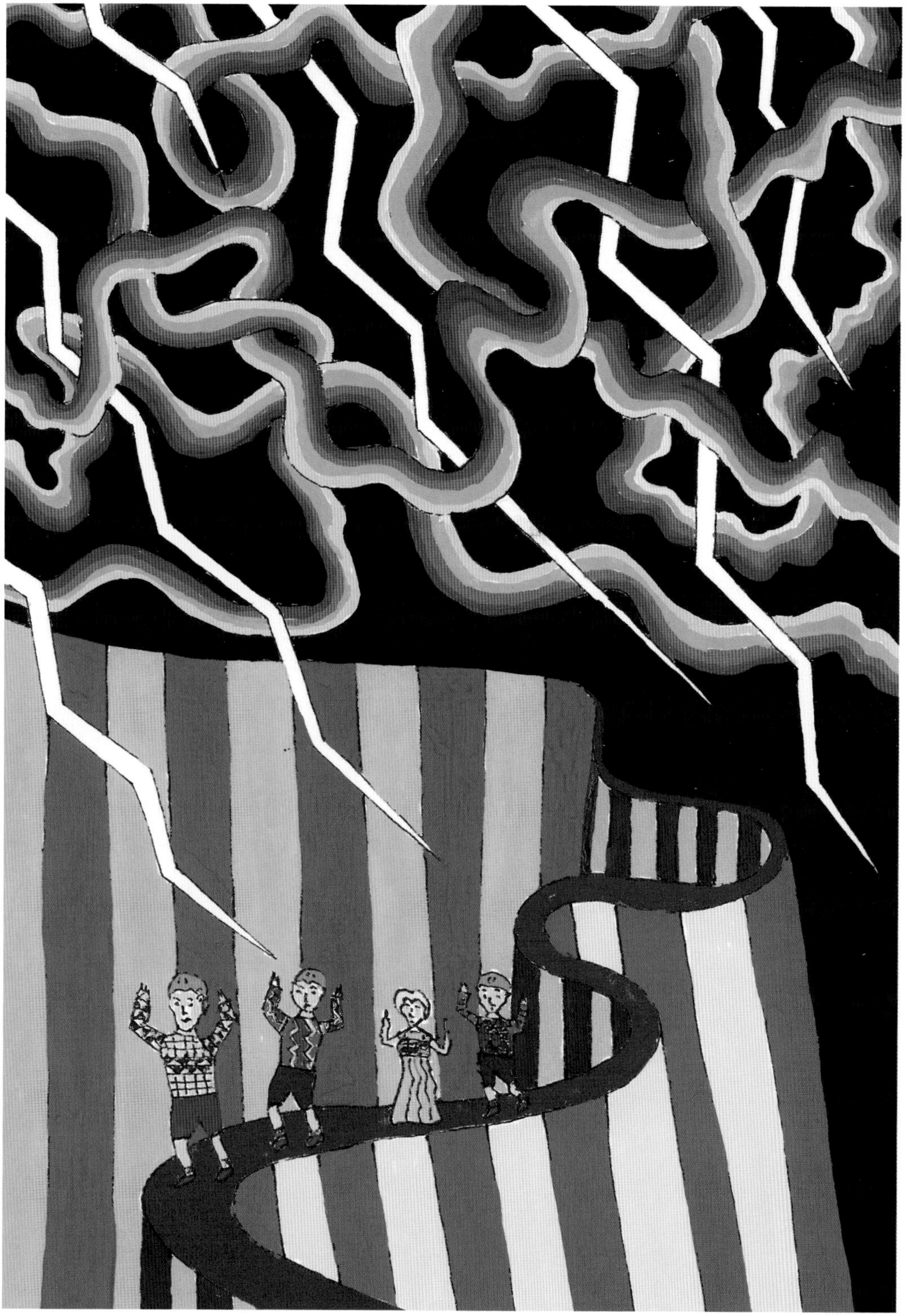

"Trust in Snuggle," whispered Benje in Susan's ear as the cat breathed on them and the boys jumped off the edge taking Susan with them.

"This is fun!" shouted Susan in amazement. "Way to go!" shouted the brothers as boys, girl and cat flew through the sky, storms raging around them.

From a jungle far below huge butterflies rose into the air carrying nets. They were collectors: they wanted human specimens to pin into their collections. As they drew near to the children and cat they swished their nets through the air. Julius ducked. He felt the movement of the nets pass over his head. "Snuggle! That felt real! I thought you said that in the Place of Nightmares there is nothing to fear but fear itself."

"I did, but something is wrong. The Nightmares have become real! It must be the Princess of the Night." So saying Snuggle unsheathed his claws (they glinted in the rising sun). With a mighty battle cry the cat slashed the nets of the butterflies, who flew off moaning loudly, "Unfair! Unfair!" "Damned Dream Lord!" "No specimens to pin into our collections!"

The boys, cat and Susan had not flown much further when Julius spied distant specks on the horizon flying towards them. "What are they?" he asked.

Snuggle had very good eyesight. Even he was shocked at what he saw. "Huge game birds carrying shotguns!" he cried.

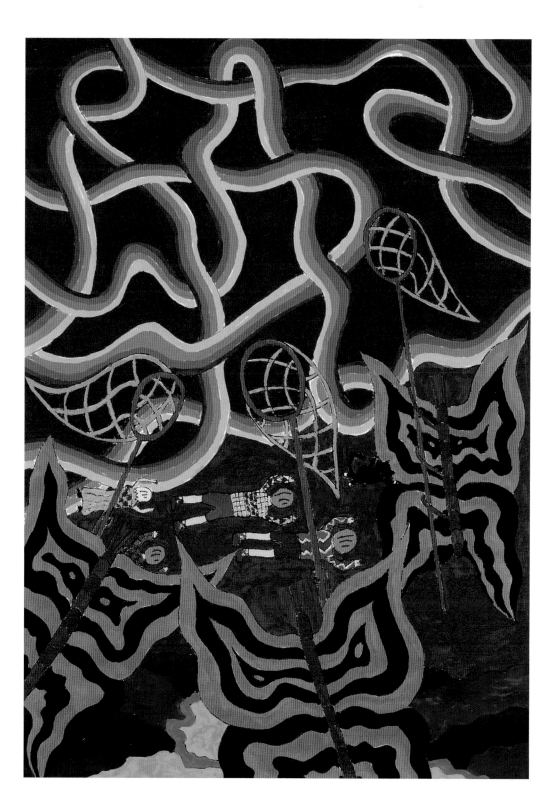

It was the hunting season in the Place of Nightmares. The boys did not like the idea of being hunted (whether by game birds with shotguns or butterflies with nets). What was worse they knew their mother had a phobia of birds.

Julius whispered anxiously in Snuggle's ear, "Mum is frightened of birds. If they get near she will freeze. In her panic she will not be able to fly."

"Then I had better engage those birds in battle," said Snuggle calmly. "Go and shelter in the jungle."

So saying Snuggle let out a mighty battle cry, changed into a creature half man half cat with sword and shield in hand, and flew towards the game birds. The battle was short and sharp. The birds fired their guns, but squawked in dismay as the bullets bounced off Snuggle's shield or Snuggle caught the bullets in his teeth (this was showing off). The birds realised that it is best not to attack a Dream Lord. Swiftly they flew off.

In the meantime the boys and Susan had landed in a lake just beneath a waterfall. Susan was a very good swimmer. Soon she was trying to persuade the boys to join her on a swimming expedition across the lake (even though the lake was vast).

"Just like Mum," sighed the boys.

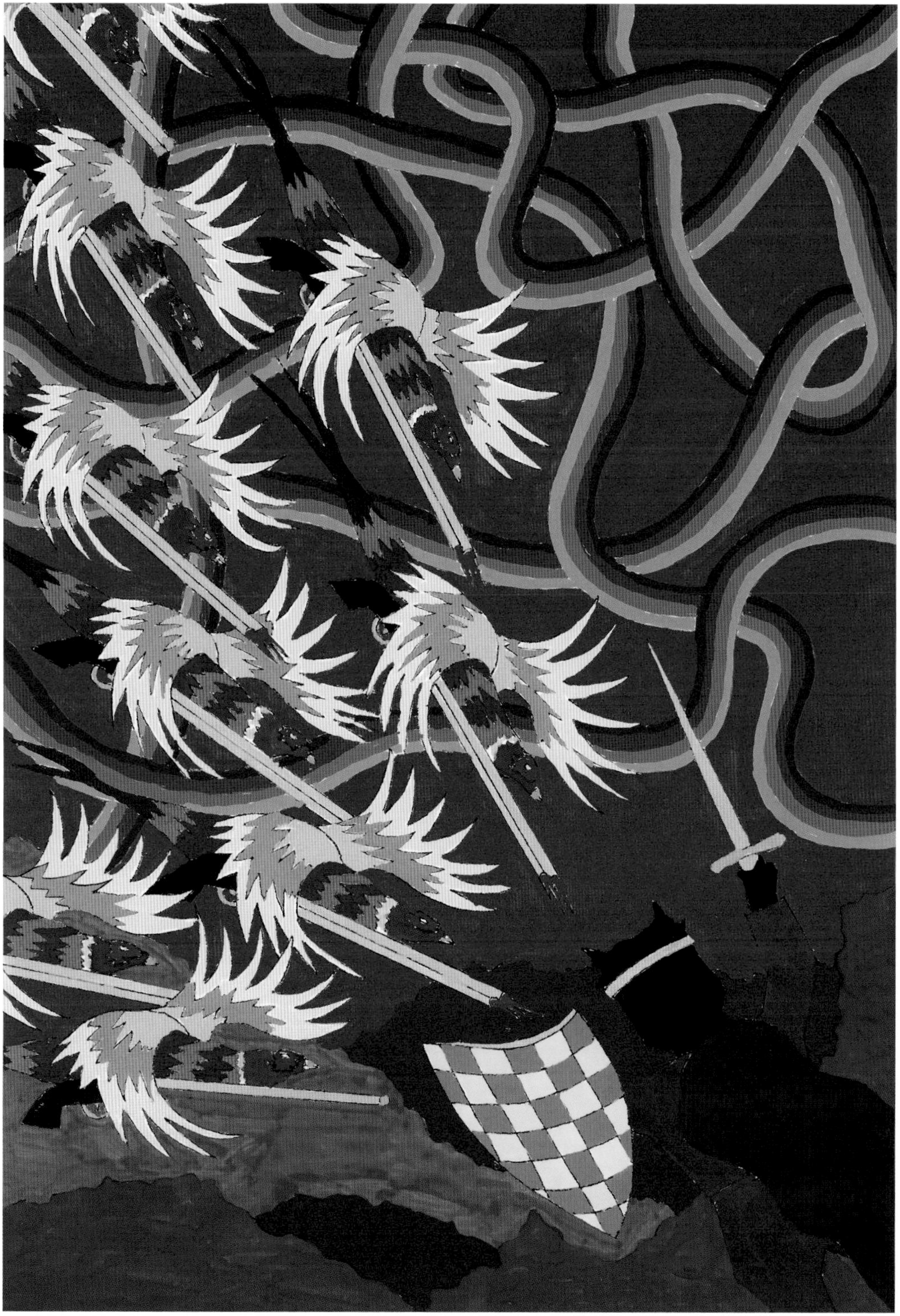

Then the boys saw food floating in the air just above the water: grapes, bananas, even Marmite sandwiches for Alexander. The boys were starving. They were just about to reach up and eat the food when Susan shouted out a warning, "There are fish at the top of the waterfall. They are fishing!"

The boys swam back from the bottom of the waterfall and looking up gasped in horror. At the top were huge fish with fishing rods and lines with food as bait, hoping to catch a boy or girl.

At that moment Snuggle arrived. Still half man half cat he slashed the lines with his sword and the food fell into the grateful hands of the boys and girl. Susan and the brothers were pleased, but the fish were not.

"Damned Dream Lord!" squeaked the fish baring their teeth, wishing they could have a girl or boy to eat.

"In our adventures someone nearly always wants to eat us," Julius informed Susan coolly.

"What exciting lives you lead!" the girl replied, full of admiration.

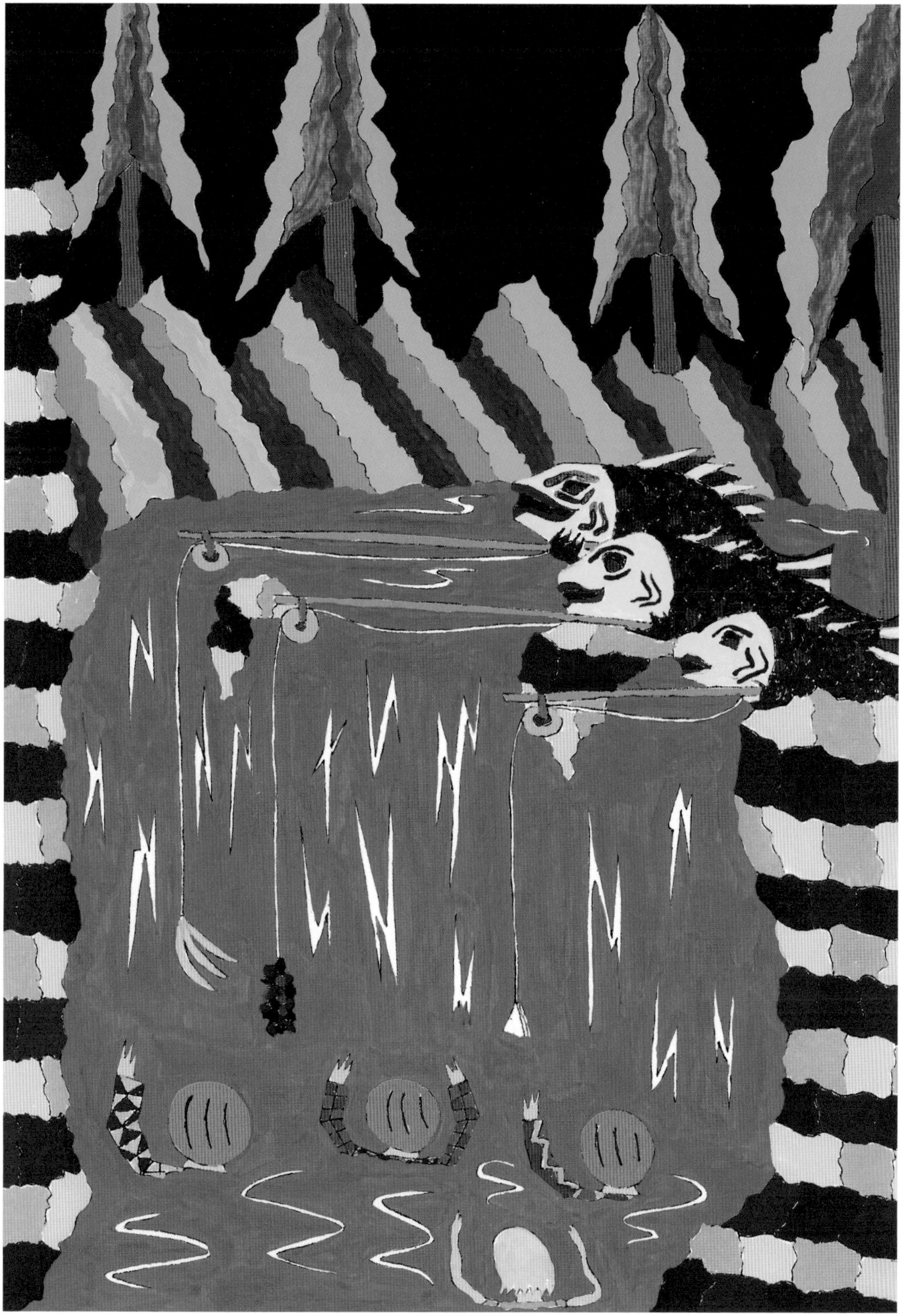

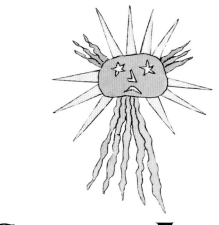

CHAPTER FOUR

After the boys and Susan had eaten well they began to float downstream on their backs. "Soon we shall reach an entrance to the Land of Dreams," said Snuggle. Every now and then a great fanged monster would rear up out of the water and bare its teeth. At first the boys and girl screamed and screamed, but when they realised that these nightmare monsters were not real they laughed, stuck out their tongues and cried "Yah! Boo! Sucks!" until the monsters got fed up and disappeared.

The boys, girl and Snuggle had not floated far when they saw a rocky cliff and in the cliff a cave, the entrance barred by a door. "The way into the Land of Dreams!" cried Snuggle as he became once more a cat and led them out of the stream.

All were dripping wet, but Snuggle opening his mouth and breathing out hot air dried first himself, then Susan and the brothers.

"Your cat is marvellous!" said Susan admiringly. "First he defeats butterflies, birds and fish. Then he turns himself into a hair drier!"

After all were dry, boys girl and cat walked to the entrance to the Land of Dreams.

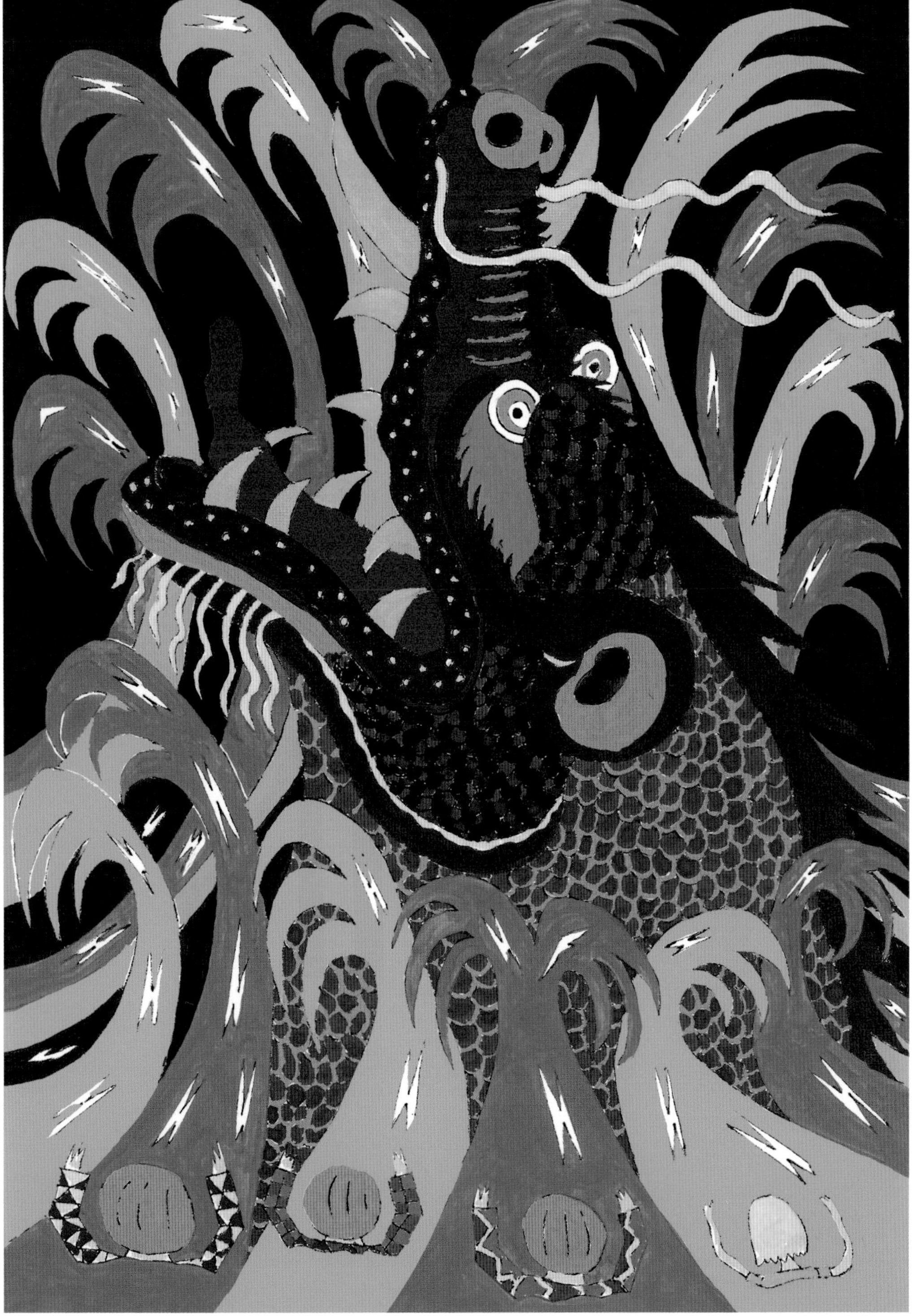

At the entrance there was a little dream. He was not happy. The door was locked. He could not get in. "What sort of dream are you?" asked Julius.

"A Dream of Destiny." "Destiny!" chorused Julius and Alex scornfully, for the dream was very pale and small and looked pretty pathetic.

But Benjamin did not join in the scorn. Julius had his dream of words. Alex had his dream of painting. Ben had no special dream. He wanted one. "How did you get here?" Benjamin asked Little Dream.

"Like other Dreams of Destiny I was given to a child at his birth. I liked him. I thought that we would grow together. But he was only interested in playing football for Manchester United."

"Nearly all boys want to be football stars when we are young," observed Julius. "Man U, Arsenal, Barcelona or Real Madrid. But we grow out of it."

"Most do. But this boy did not," replied Little Dream. "All he wanted to do was kick a ball. So on the Night of Dreams I decided to return to the dream realm hoping that one day I will go back to earth in the breast of a child who is interested in me. But when I got to the Arrivals Hall everything was in confusion and by mistake I took the exit to the Place of Nightmares. I have had a wretched time. Now at last I have reached the entrance to the Land of Dreams I cannot get in."

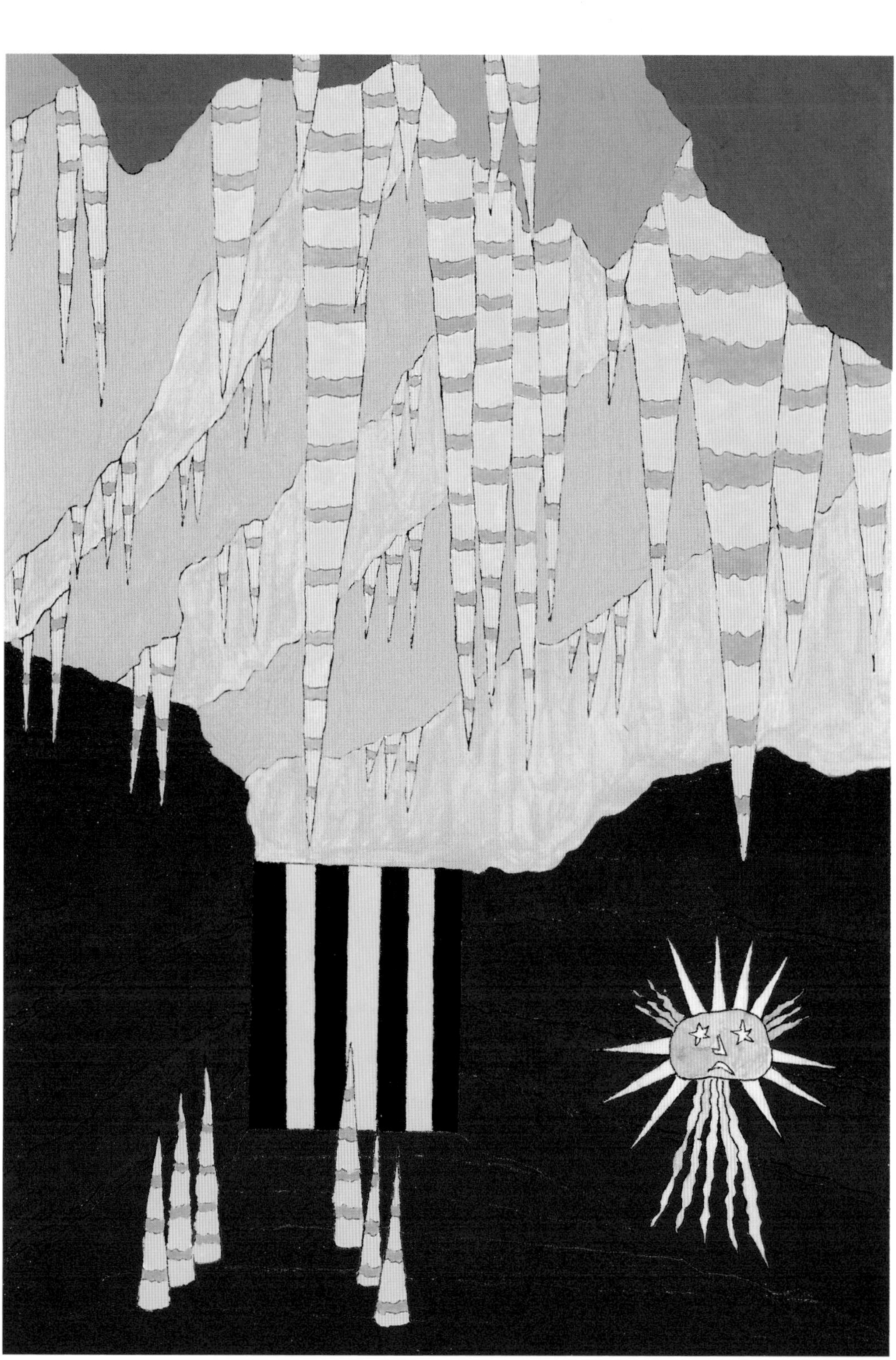

Benjamin whispered in the ear of Little Dream, "What is your dream?" In a whisper the dream told him. "Then you will be my dream. But we will not tell my brothers the nature of your dream. I want it to be our secret." At this Little Dream began to look more happy.

"But what about my dream?" asked Susan loudly. "I am glad that Ben has found a dream, but I thought that we were going to recover my dream from the Dream Thief."

"We are," replied Snuggle gravely. "But more is at stake than just your dream. The Dream Thief is a friend of the Princess of the Night. He has stolen many dreams. With the loss of every dream the pool of dreams becomes less, and the universe contracts."

"If many dreams have been stolen why have you come with the boys to rescue mine?" asked Susan.

"What is special in this case is not your dream, but that of Alexander," replied Snuggle.

"Mine!" gasped Alex.

"How can that be?" asked Susan beginning to suspect that something was being kept hidden from her.

Snuggle took a deep breath and turning to the boys said, "I have to tell her." "Tell me what?" "These are your sons. When you grow up your first born will be Julius, middle child Alex, youngest Benje."

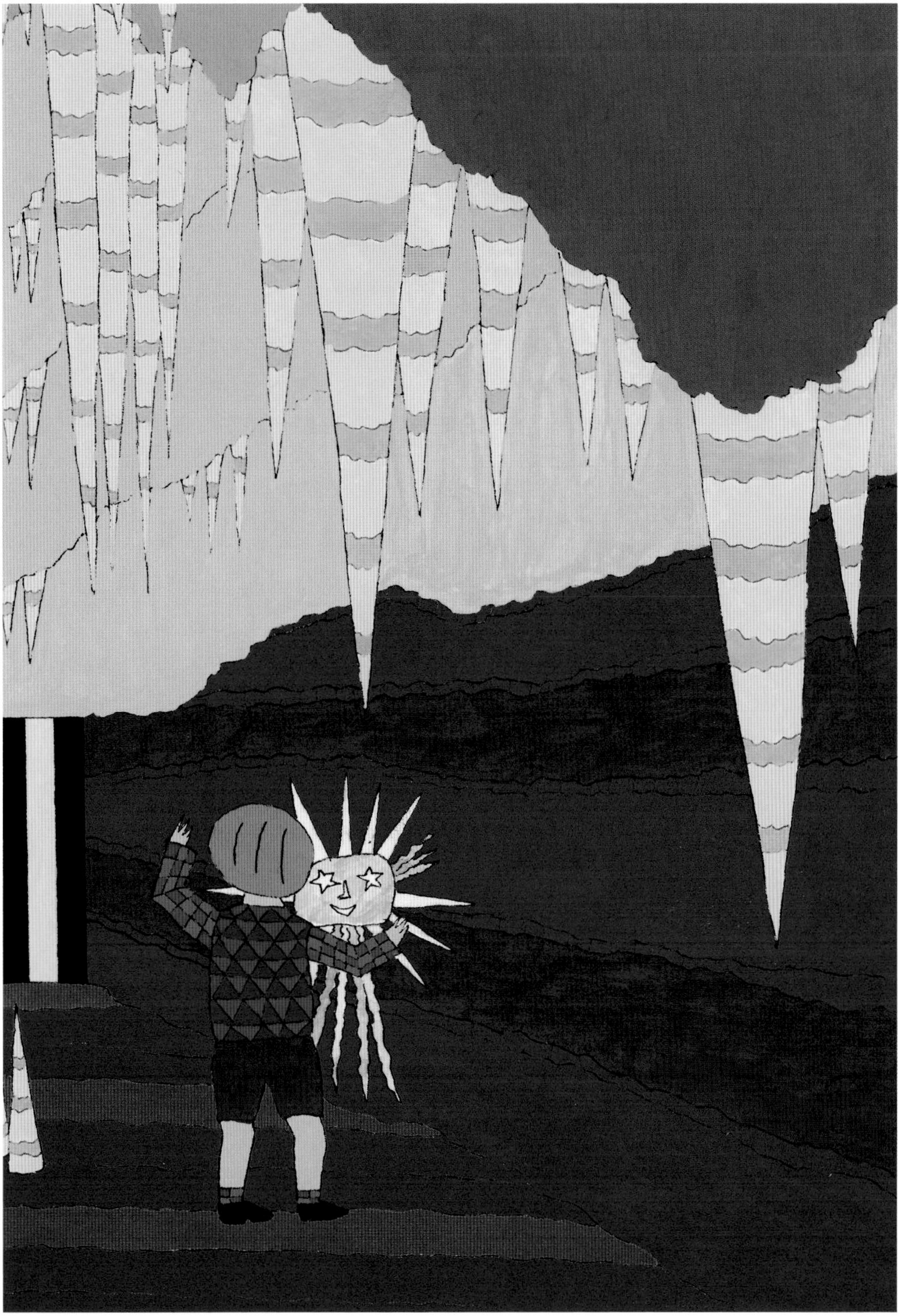

"We did not want to tell you because we feared it might freak you out," said Alex. "It does." "But also because we are afraid," added Julius. "Afraid of what?"

"Afraid that you might not like us." "Afraid you might decide not to have children." "Afraid we might never come into existence."

Susan turned to Snuggle: "But what is so special about Alex's dream?" "Alex's dream is special because it is exactly the same as yours." "How so?"

"When he was born your dream split in two. One half stayed with you. The other half entered Alexander. With the help of Alex's dream we shall be able to track down your dream, free it from the Dream Thief and hopefully free the dreams of others. But we have talked too long. It is time for action."

So saying Snuggle raised his arm and the door to the Land of Dreams sprang open. The cat, boys, girl and Little Dream entered the cave.

Only Snuggle and Little Dream could see in the dark. Snuggle led the way, a silver aura round his body ("It must be because he is a Dream Lord," whispered Julius to his brothers). Specks of silver light began to shine around the cavern like glow worms waking and stretching after a long sleep.

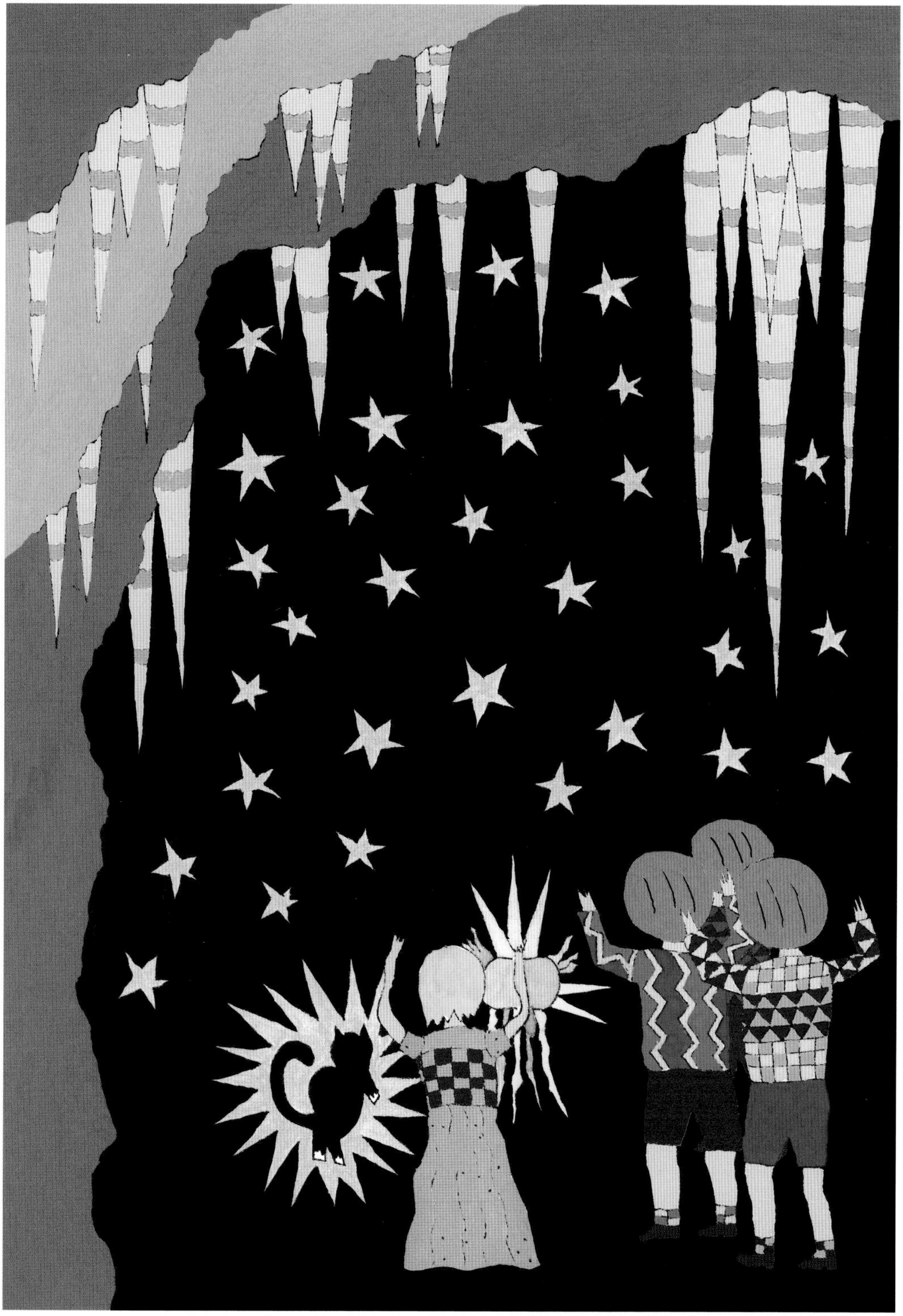

The specks of light began to change to green, then red, then gold, to form patterns of shimmering light. Each child saw a different scene: only Snuggle saw the dreams of all. The scenes changed and merged and Susan and the boys stood spellbound before the sight of their lives as they might be.

"Is that my future?" asked Julius.

"It might be," replied the cat. "But nothing is fixed and dreams can be true or false. This cave is not safe for mortals. I should not have brought you here," he added looking at the boys and girl wide-eyed and transfixed by the sights of what might be, their spirits beginning to rise up out of their bodies and merge with the images about them.

Swiftly Snuggle breathed upon the children, cried, "Hold hands, shut eyes and follow me," and led the way through the cave until they emerged above a forest.

The children opened their eyes to see a land of shimmering colours, everything more brilliant, more intense than back on earth. Their hearts felt lighter, the grass a brighter green, and when they walked upon the grass it had a bounce and spring that caused them to rise up in the air and gambol like lambs.

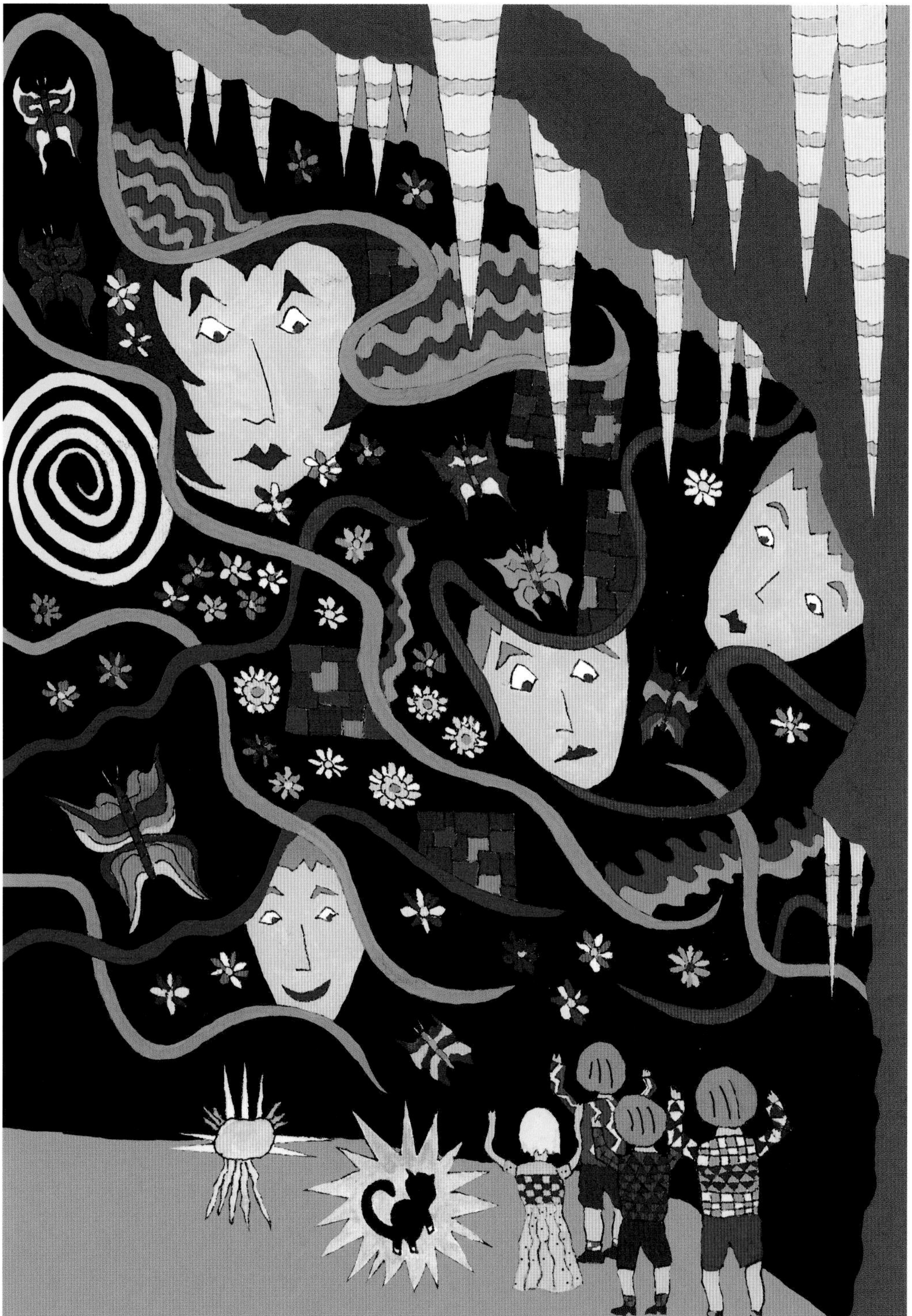

CHAPTER FIVE

"Alex," said Snuggle turning to the boy. "We need your dream to lead us. May I take it from your body?"

Alex hesitated: "I might lose my dream. Like Mum."

"True, but the whole universe is in danger of losing its dreams. That would be the end of life as anyone would wish to live it."

"Then take my dream."

Snuggle moved his arm and mouthed a gentle invocation. Alex's dream emerged sheepishly from his body, blinking in the sunlight. "Greetings Dream Lord," said the dream bowing low before the cat. "I can feel Susan's dream, my other half. I shall lead you to her."

Alex's dream led the way deeper and deeper into the Land of Dreams. The scenery changed without a moment's notice. One moment they were in a forest which seemed to go on for ever, then a desert where sand stretched out around them as far as the eye could see, then the white sand turned to snow and soaring mountain peaks rose up from which hung castles and cathedrals of blue ice. But through all the changes Alex's dream knew precisely which way to go.

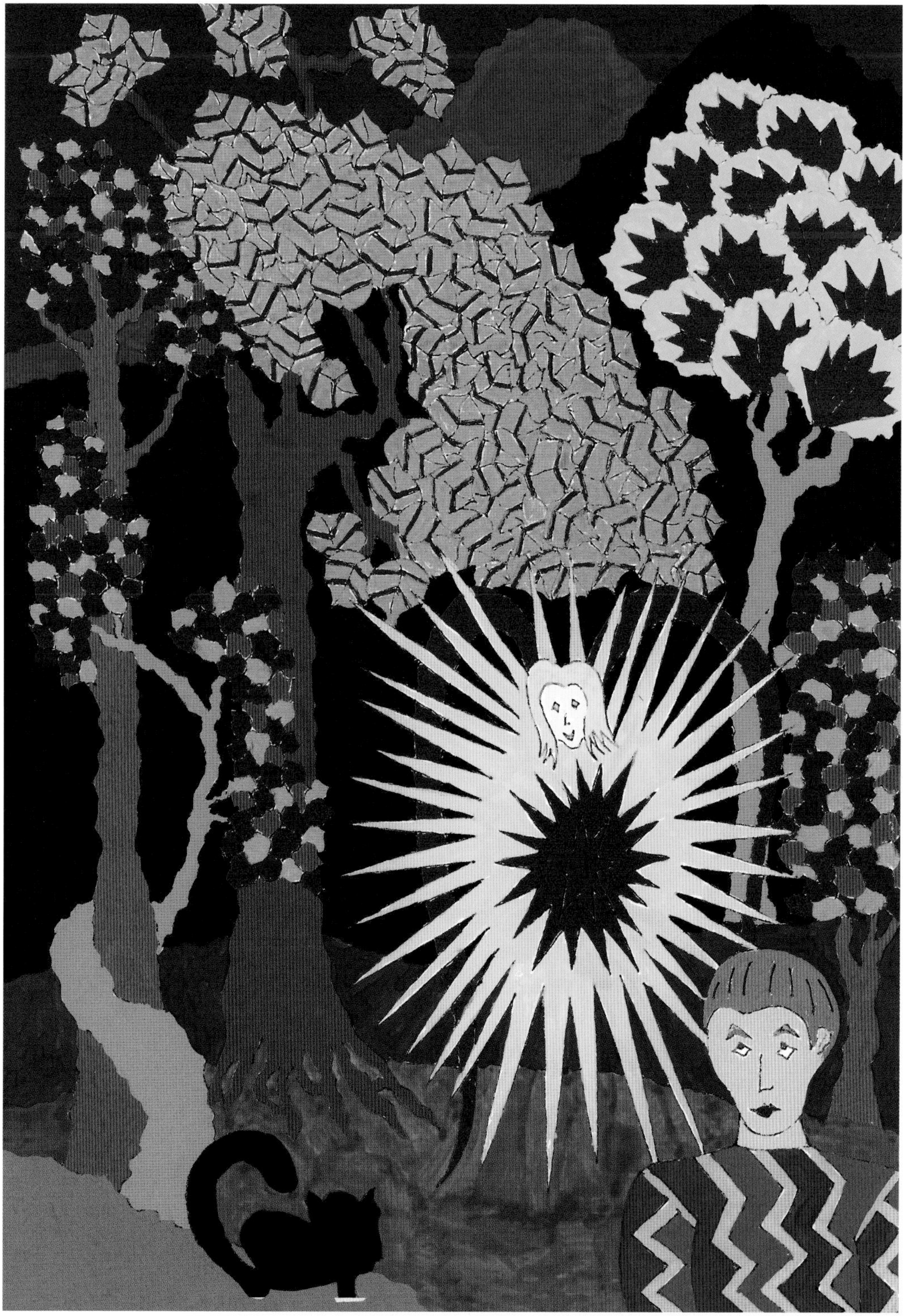

When the children were tired they lay down and slumber dreams flew to them covering their bodies with golden wings. Instantly they fell asleep waking only minutes later completely refreshed.

Deep inside a forest the children found a grove of dreamfruit hanging from trees of gold and silver. Each child only had to raise an arm and fruit would fly to the outstretched hand, fruit which was perfectly ripe, good and tasting of whatever the child wanted to eat.

"Great Marmite-tasting apples!" murmured Alex.

"The chocolate-tasting ones are far nicer!" replied Susan.

Every now and then a dream would approach Susan and ask if it could be her dream. Politely she declined: "I must remain true to my special dream." But one dream kept its distance and followed Susan secretly.

Snuggle was always on guard, looking this way and that. He knew they would be attacked. The only question was when and where. Then the attack came. Between the trees streamed the mighty Gnargs, servants of the Princess of the Night in seething shades of blue and grey, holding flails of deep despair.

But Snuggle felt no fear. He turned to face them, changed into a creature half man half cat, and with sword and shield in hand he drove them back (though he was one against many).

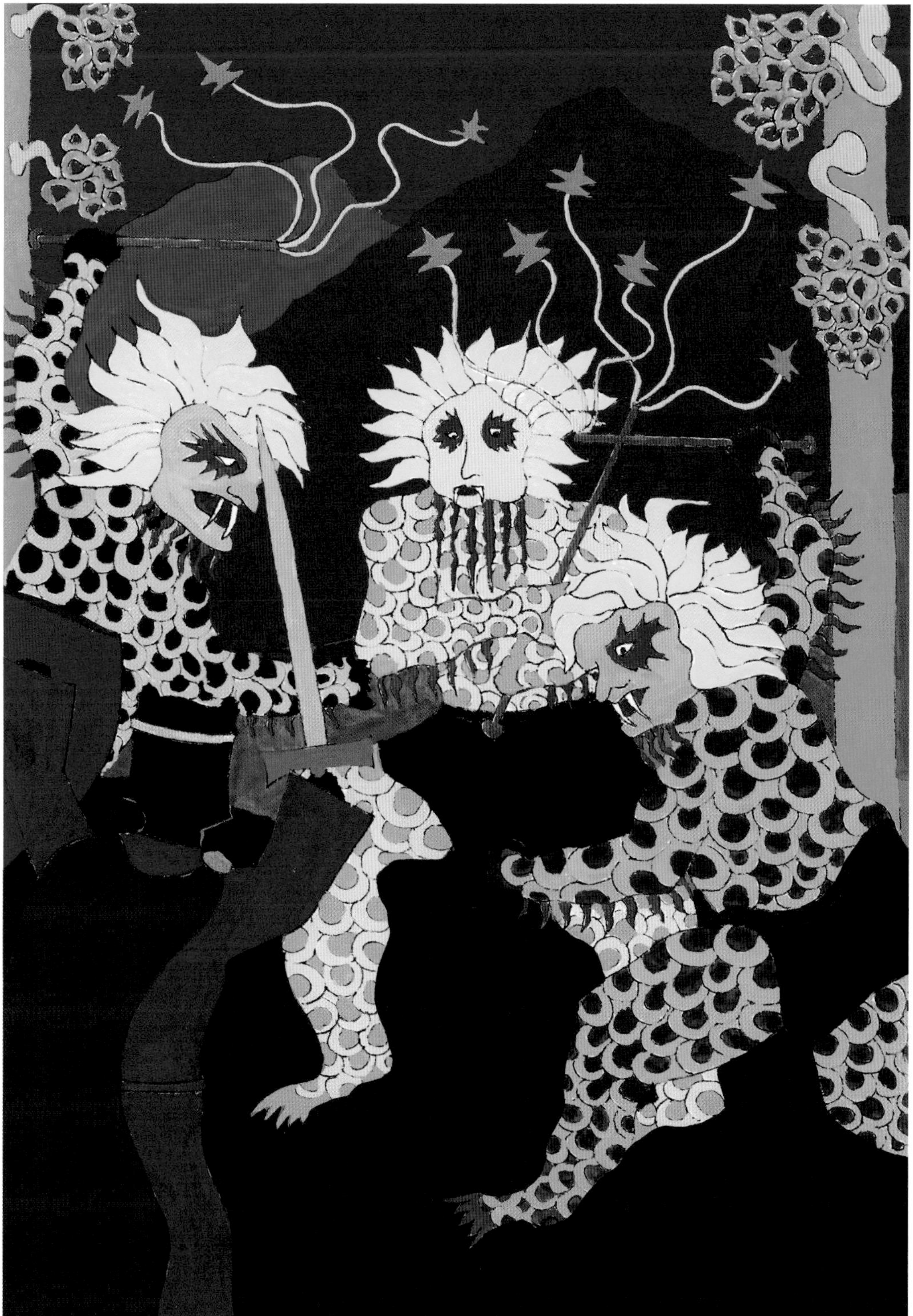

Snuggle did not see (until too late) the Princess of the Night fly in from the other side in the guise of a great bat. She swooped. She was interested in only one thing. She grasped Alex's dream. She carried the dream off before Snuggle could stop her. As her servants retreated even the cat felt a momentary pang of fear.

"My dream! My dream!" gasped Alex. "The Princess has got it."

"How can we find my dream now?" groaned Susan in despair.

The cat looked up. He raised his sword as if in greeting and returning it to its scabbard, replied firmly, "Keep travelling. The Gardener said before we left whatever happens in the Land of Dreams keep travelling. Never give up."

"We won't," responded the boys. "Nor me." added Susan.

"Nor me," squeaked Little Dream, "Do not forget me." All looked at Little Dream. He had become brighter and more solid. "Before Alex's dream was captured I spoke to her. She told me where the Dream Thief has hidden Susan's dream. I think I can find her."

"Then lead the way," said Snuggle.

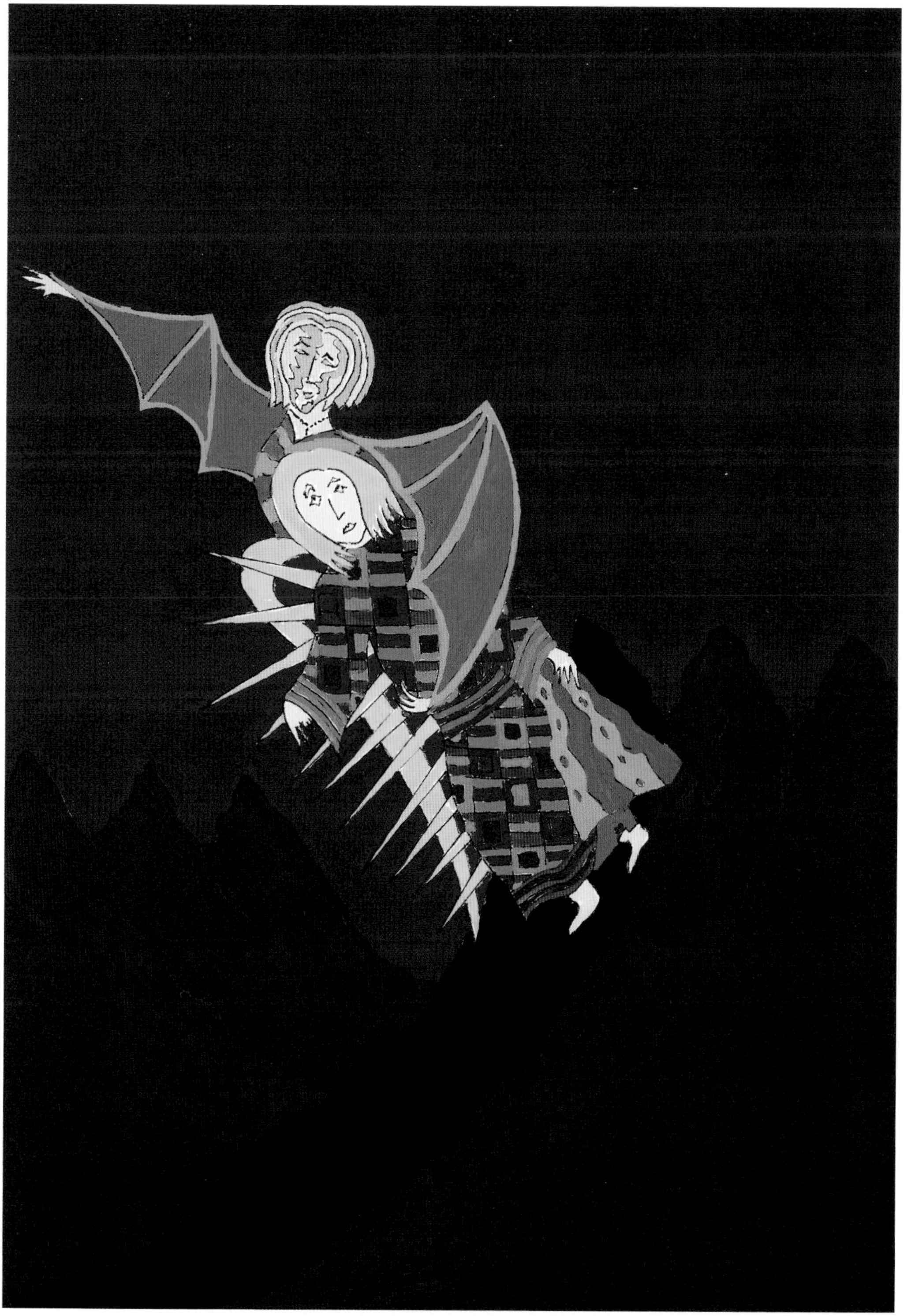

The landscape was not so bright and brilliant as it had been before the attack. The hillside where the Servants of the Night had attacked was now tinged in grey. Trees let out sad sighs as they swayed in the gusting breeze, precious fruit falling rotten to the ground. The party of travellers had not travelled far when they were joined by a company of Hero Dreamhogs (much like Hero Hedgehogs but with spines of shining light and fire in their bellies). The Hero Dreamhogs saluted smartly.

Their Captain apologised for not arriving in time to save Alex's Dream: he did not mention that in fighting their way past the Servants of the Night they had lost many of their number, their translucent colours choked by clouds of black and grey.

"Do not worry," replied Snuggle to the Captain. "Little Dream is showing us the way."

"I have something for you from the Gardener," said the Captain. He handed Snuggle a package. It was as light as a feather dancing in the breeze.

Snuggle nodded gravely as he opened the package and a little plant with a silver aura jumped out. "A Precious Plant in the form of a dream! I have never seen one before. No doubt like other Precious Plants it has the power to reverse evil magic. What is the message?"

"You are to give Precious Dream Plant to Little Dream."

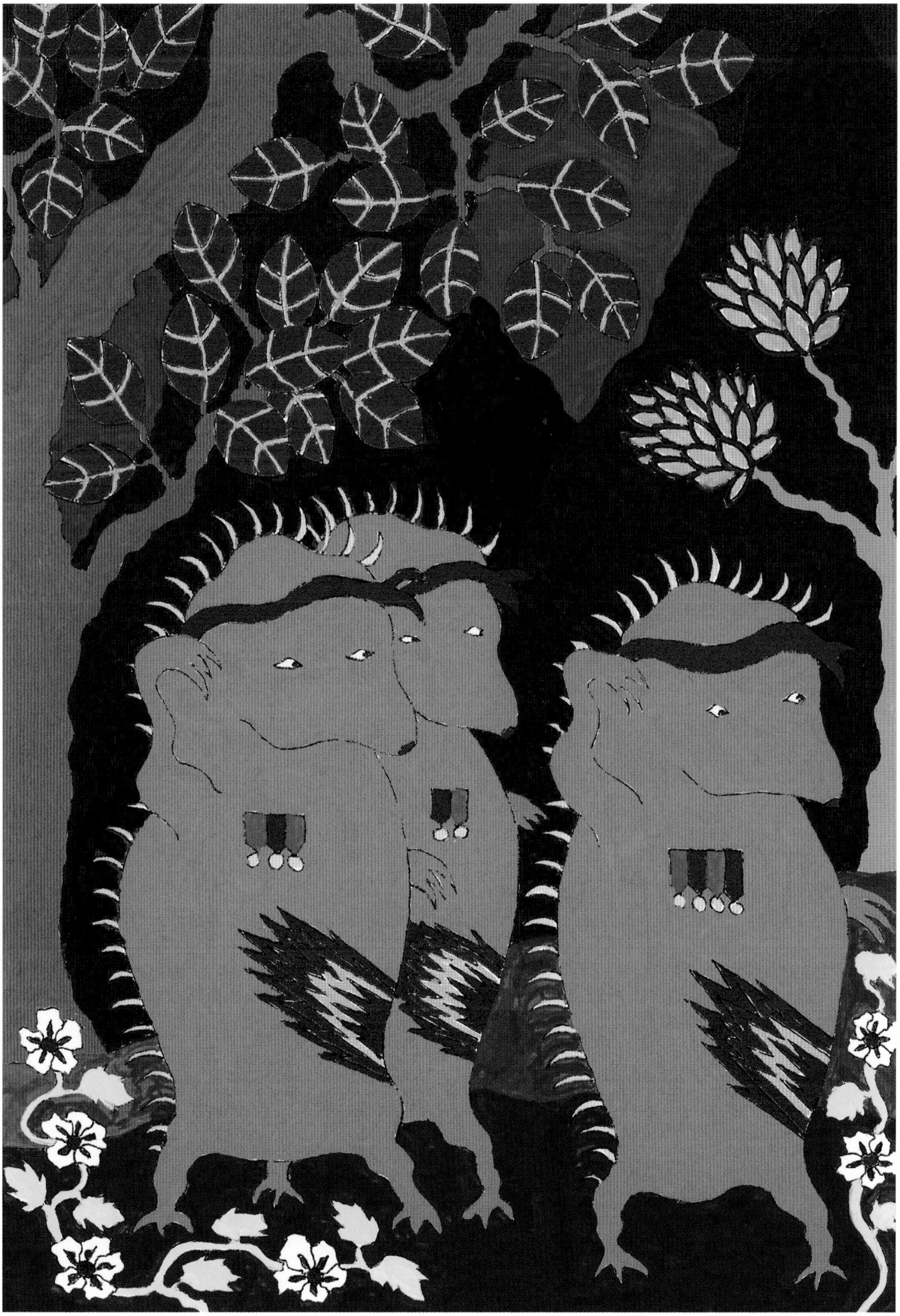

Snuggle smiled, a knowing smile of understanding. Raising his paw he drew on all his powers as Dream Lord and with words of invocation hid Precious Dream Plant deep within the breast of Little Dream.

Snuggle then divided the Hero Dreamhogs into two, the vanguard at the front, the rear guard to guard the rear. The Captain carried a horn to sound in case of attack.

As the party travelled deeper into the Land of Dreams, Ben walked with Little Dream, Susan and Alex hand in hand, both burdened by the loss of their dream.

All travelled in silence until Snuggle decided they needed cheering up and started to sing the ballad of "Cuddles the Conqueror", a warrior cat of old. The noise was ghastly. Everyone asked Snuggle (quite politely) would he please shut up.

The party passed sights of great beauty, a city of turrets and walls which seemed to move, to soar up into the sky, then disappear into the earth. But when they asked Little Dream if the city was the stronghold of the Dream Thief the dream murmured no and they continued on their way.

Billowing clouds of black and grey drew closer from the rear. Every now and then the horn would sound as servants of the Princess of the Night attacked, always from the rear, never from the front, as the party was drawn deeper into the Land of Dreams.

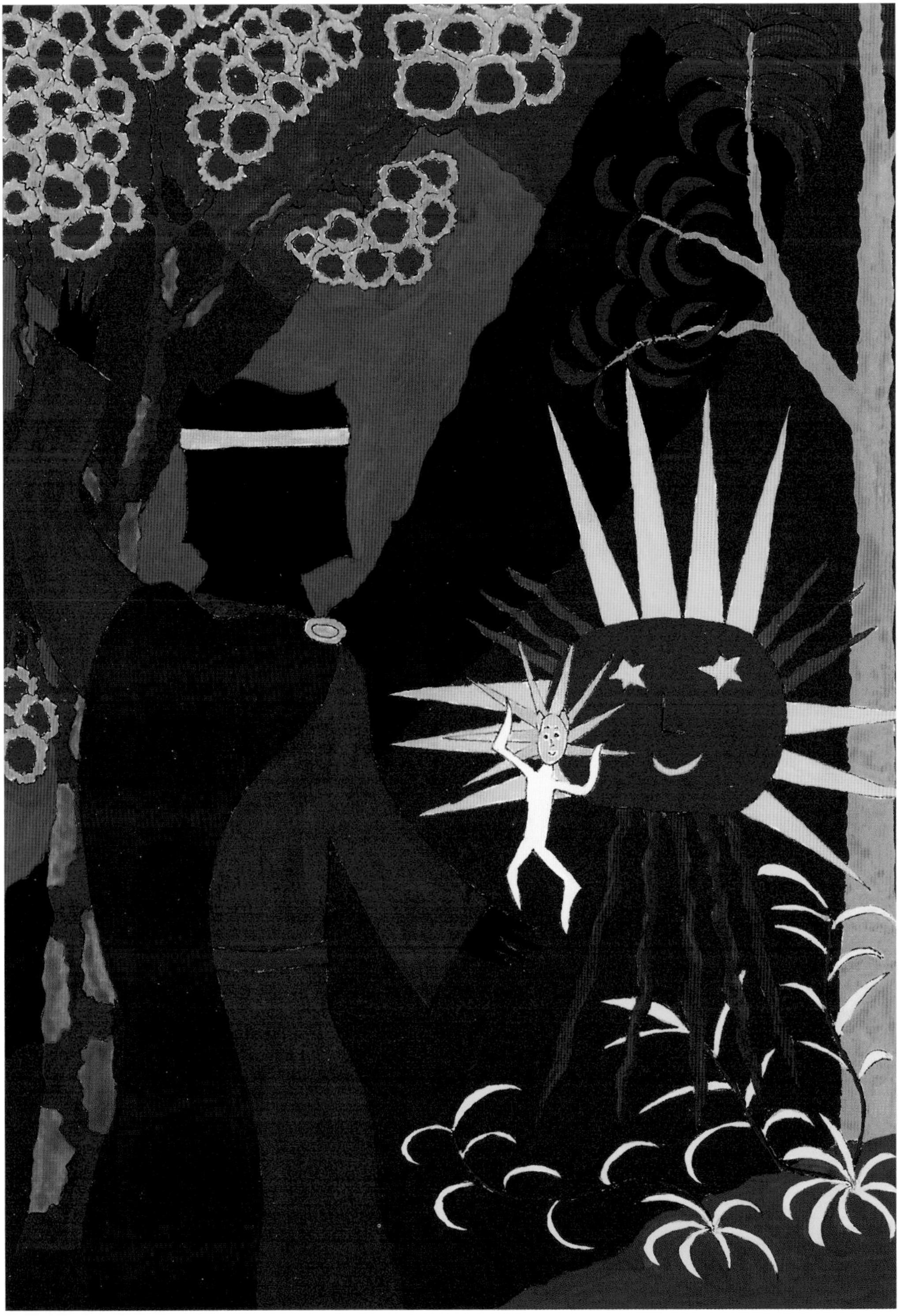

When the horn sounded Snuggle longed to take his sword and join the Hero Dreamhogs in the fight, but he knew he must remain beside the boys, girl and Little Dream and protect them from attack. With each attack the number of Hero Dreamhogs became fewer, but they never complained or showed any sign of fear.

Emerging from a forest the party reached a narrow bridge of glass soaring high into the sky above a river of molten lava. Behind them, the clouds of billowing darkness drew ever closer as the Hero Dreamhogs tried in vain to keep the Servants of the Night at bay. The Captain sounded his horn for the last time.

All remaining Hero Dreamhogs (from front and rear) gathered around their Captain. At his command they formed a semi-circle around the entrance to the bridge, to hold the bridge at whatever cost until Snuggle could lead the boys, girl and Little Dream safely to the other side.

At once a vast horde of Servants of the Night attacked, spitting, hissing, turning everything they touched to grey. The Hero Dreamhogs fired spines of translucent light from their bodies, trying in vain to keep the darkness at bay as their life light began to ebb away.

Snuggle, the children and Little Dream had not quite reached the other side when the last of the translucent light was extinguished, and a billowing cloud of darkness began to sweep across the bridge.

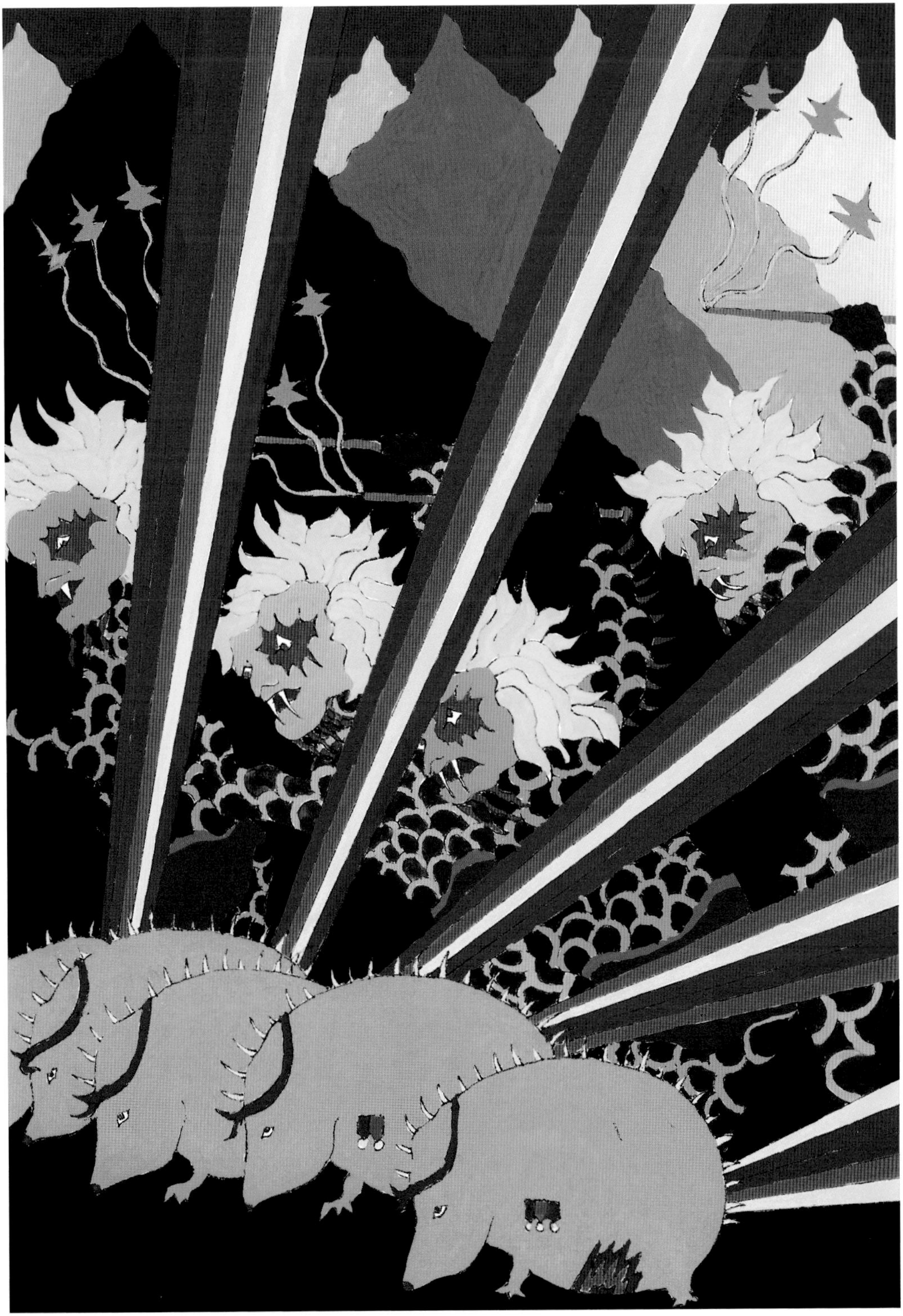

Chapter Six

As the children and Little Dream jumped off the bridge Snuggle calmly raised his sword and with a battle cry called upon the Gardener and all the powers of light to give him strength. With great rhythmic blows of his sword he began to cut through the struts which supported the bridge.

As the first strut cracked the bridge began to sway and a moan rose up from the cloud of darkness rushing onward to kill the cat. As the second strut cracked the bridge broke free and disappeared (with the cloud of darkness) into the molten lava. Just before the bridge broke free the secret dream jumped clear.

Snuggle led the way up a gorge cut deep into high rock. The gorge twisted and turned with smaller gorges disappearing on both sides. Once it had been a place of bright delight, greeting passing travellers with the sight of strange animals, fruit and vegetation which had long disappeared from the rest of creation. Now everything was tinged in grey.

At every turn there was a sight which caused the children to cry out in horror. They passed a grove of dreamfruit, but all was rotten. They passed the Dream Unicorn, the most beautiful and rarest of the creatures of creation. It was staked by its wings to the earth. As Snuggle bent to free it the Dream Unicorn quietly sighed and died.

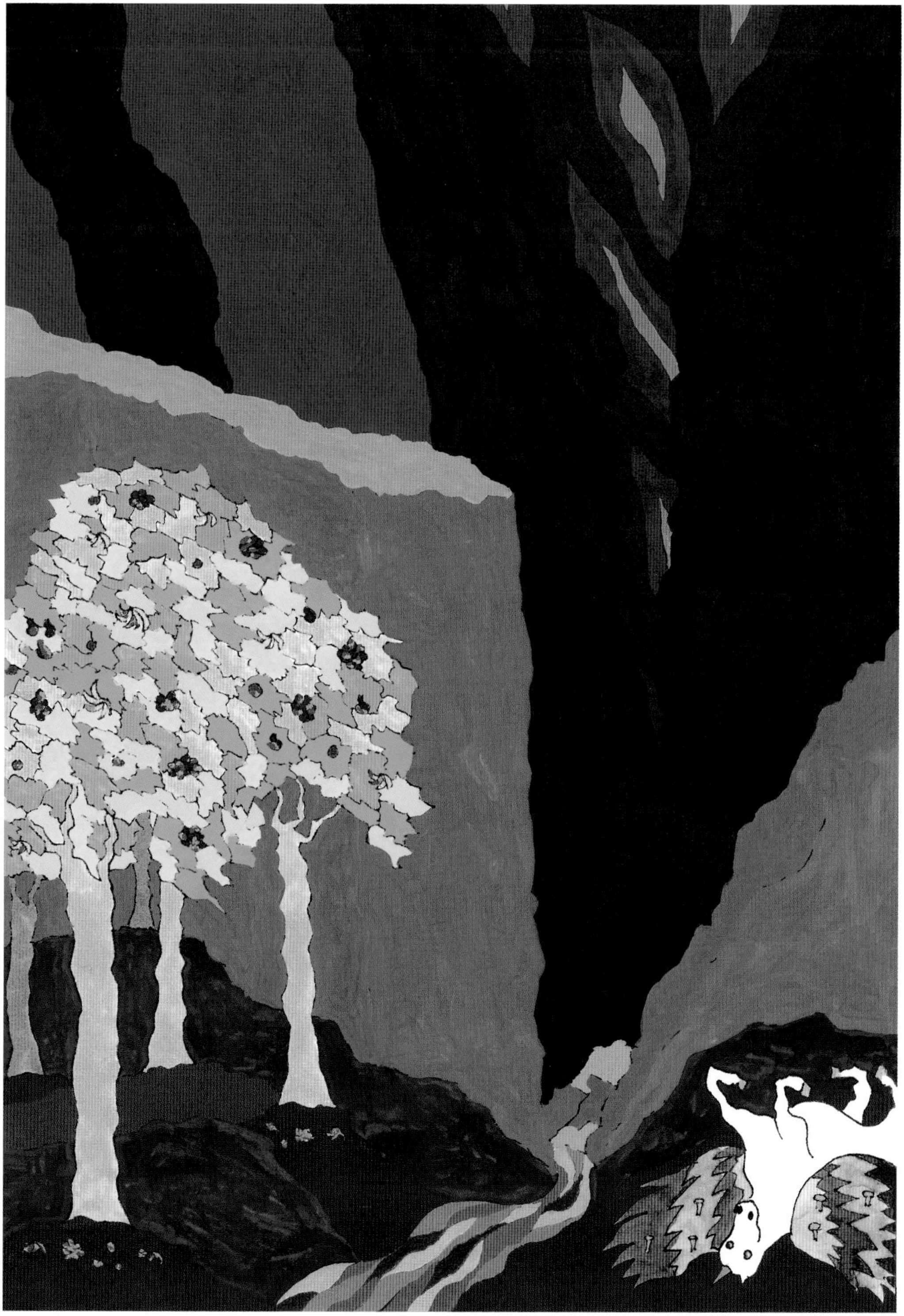

The children passed dreams, but all were crippled with broken wings unable to fly, tinged with black and grey or false and seeking to lead them to destruction. At the head of the gorge a waterfall blocked the path.

"Are you sure this is the way?" Snuggle asked Little Dream.

"A castle lies beyond the waterfall," replied Little Dream. "We must pass through it."

"Onward!" commanded Snuggle grimly leading Little Dream, the brothers and Susan through the waterfall. As they entered the waterfall the waters parted and they found themselves before the gates of a great castle on which was carved in stone the head of the Dream Thief. The stone carving opened its beak and a tongue shot out like a repulsive pink carpet. Snuggle led the way into the castle. On the wall above an inner gate stood the Dream Thief, the Princess of the Night by his side. She was laughing. He was licking his lips, rubbing his fat bouncing belly.

"Welcome to my stronghold," cried the Dream Thief. "Dream Lord throw down your sword. All come and bow low before me and my master, the Princess of the Night."

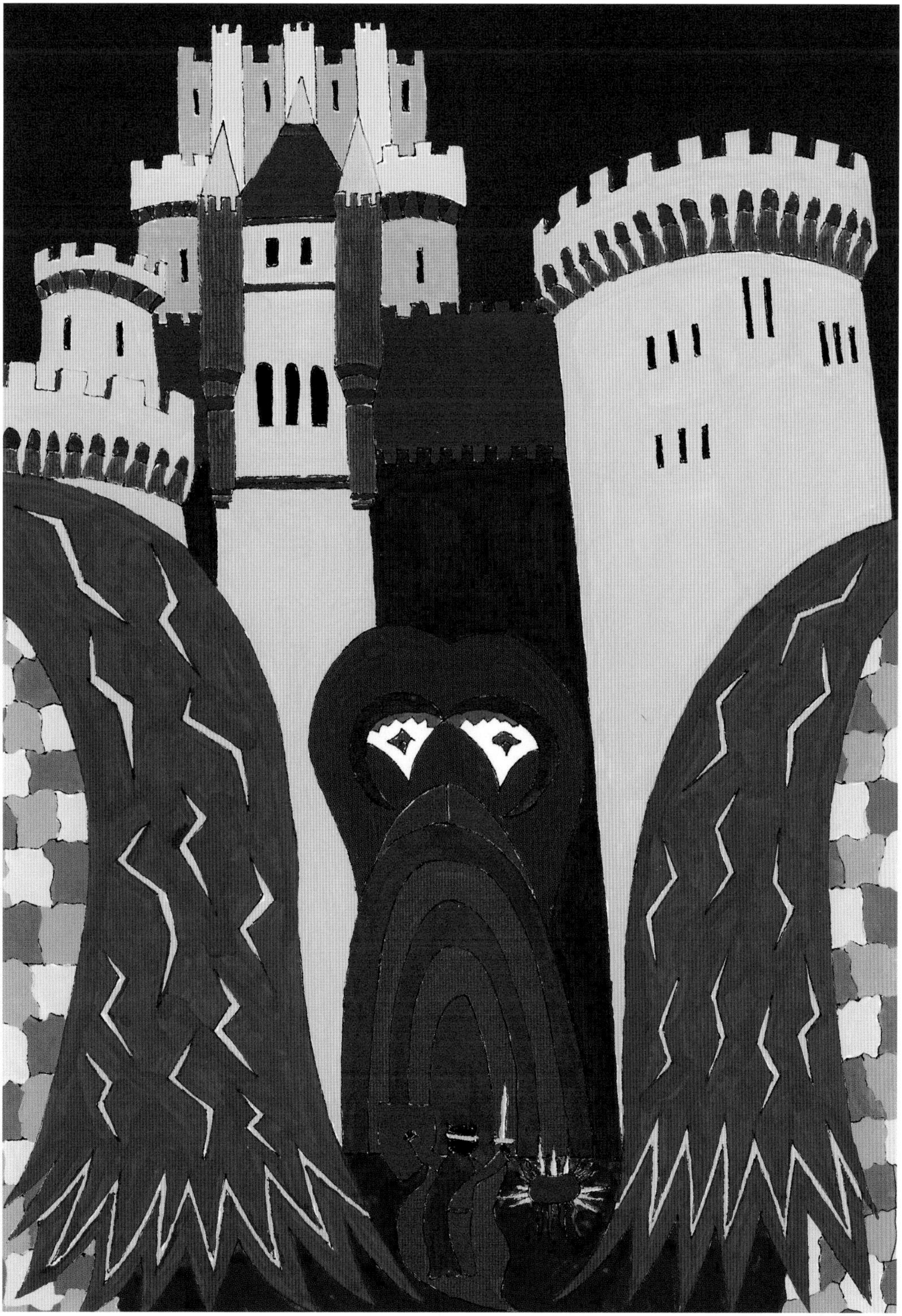

As Snuggle led the way through the inner gate a great net landed on the cat and bound him up. Then guards of the Dream Thief seized the boys, girl and Little Dream. They brought them with Snuggle to the Dream Thief and the Princess of the Night in the central keep of the castle.

The Dream Thief was particularly pleased to see Little Dream. "A Dream of Destiny," he cried excitedly as his long snaking tongue shot out and gave Little Dream a lick.

Little Dream shrank in disgust and Benje shouted angrily, "Do not touch my dream! Leave him alone!"

The Dream Thief ignored the boy and continued, "Though this dream is small and pathetic I shall enjoy sucking out his magic essence. But before I do, let me show you how this dream will spend the rest of eternity."

So saying the Dream Thief led the way down into a vast cavern deep beneath the castle. From the roof of the cavern hung the husks of Dreams of Destiny. All colour, life and brightness had been sucked out of them.

"Are those dreams?" asked the boys in disbelief. "What happened to them?" "Where is their magic?"

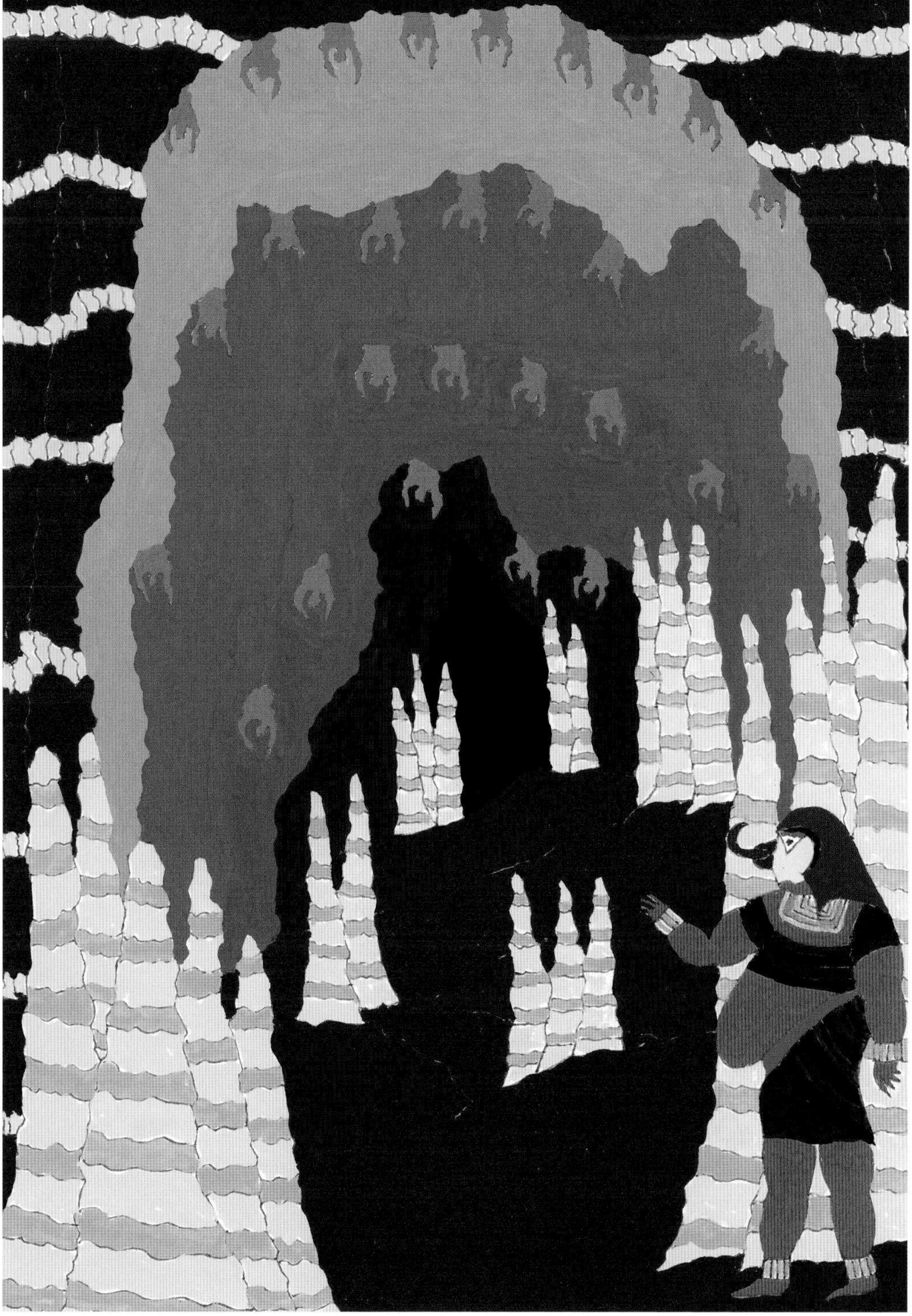

The eyes of the Dream Thief began to sparkle. He rubbed his hands. He roared with laughter. "With a magic spell I sucked in their colour, brightness and magic. It now resides within my stomach." He gave a burp and rubbed his fat belly. "I have prepared a small demonstration. I shall show you how."

At that the Dream Thief clapped his hands and servants dragged in two Dreams of Destiny bound with bands of gossamer. Each dream was identical. Having found its twin Susan's dream had regained its strength and though bound both dreams contained all the colours of the rainbow which changed and merged and changed again forming new pictures, new sculptures, a myriad of different forms of artistic creation.

"My dream!" cried Alex and Susan fearfully as they waited to see what the Dream Thief would do.

The Dream Thief and the Princess of the Night leered at the boy and girl, enjoying their discomfort. "We do hope you will enjoy seeing your dreams sucked up!"

"How dare you!" cried Susan in a very loud voice. "Let go of my dream. Give it back to me. At once."

The Dream Thief was surprised that such a little girl should have such a loud and commanding voice. But having recovered from his surprise he merely laughed, leered, rubbed his belly, and cried out, "Sucked up! Sucked up! Sucked up!"

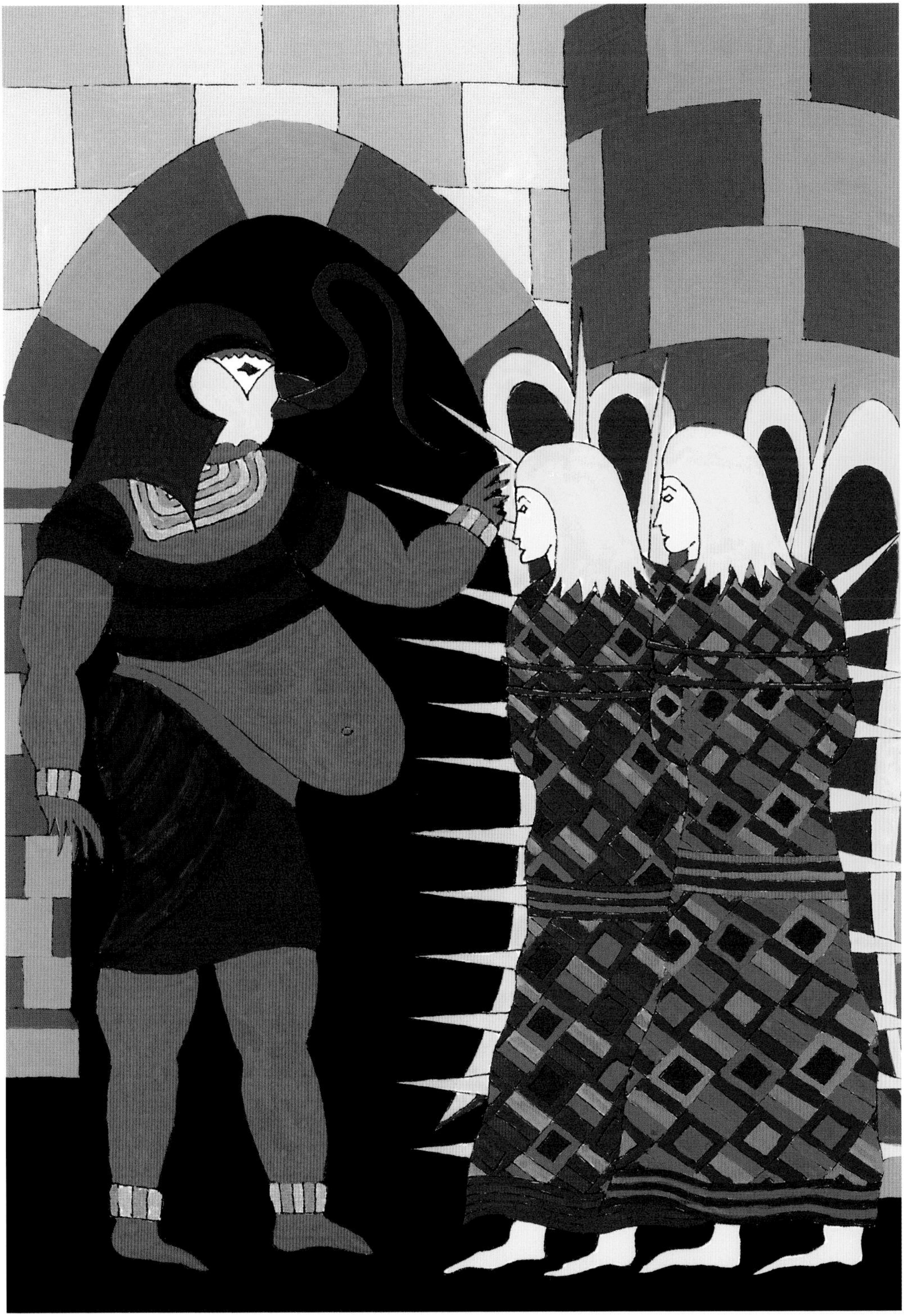

CHAPTER SEVEN

Muttering words of magic the long tongue of the Dream Thief shot out and sucked the life, colour and brightness from the dreams of Susan and Alexander, leaving them as colourless husks which floated in the air and joined other husks of sucked-out dreams in the roof of the cavern. The Princess of the Night clapped her hands in approval as the boy and girl screamed and screamed to see their dreams reduced to lifeless husks.

Then the Dream Thief turned to Little Dream. "Though you are small and pathetic I shall enjoy sucking you up as well." He made a burping sound.

Little Dream began to shake and shiver. Benjamin shouted indignantly, "Leave my dream alone."

The Dream Thief muttered once more the words of magic. His long tongue shot out to suck out the life, colour and brightness from Little Dream. But what happened next was surprising (or surprising to everyone except Snuggle who knew what was about to happen). As the magic reached Little Dream Precious Dream Plant buried deep within his breast reversed the evil magic and sucked the life, colour and brightness out of the belly of the Dream Thief.

"My dreams! My dreams!" screamed the Dream Thief holding his stomach as the life, colour and brightness of the dreams he had swallowed spewed out of his belly button and returned to the husks hanging from the roof of the cavern.

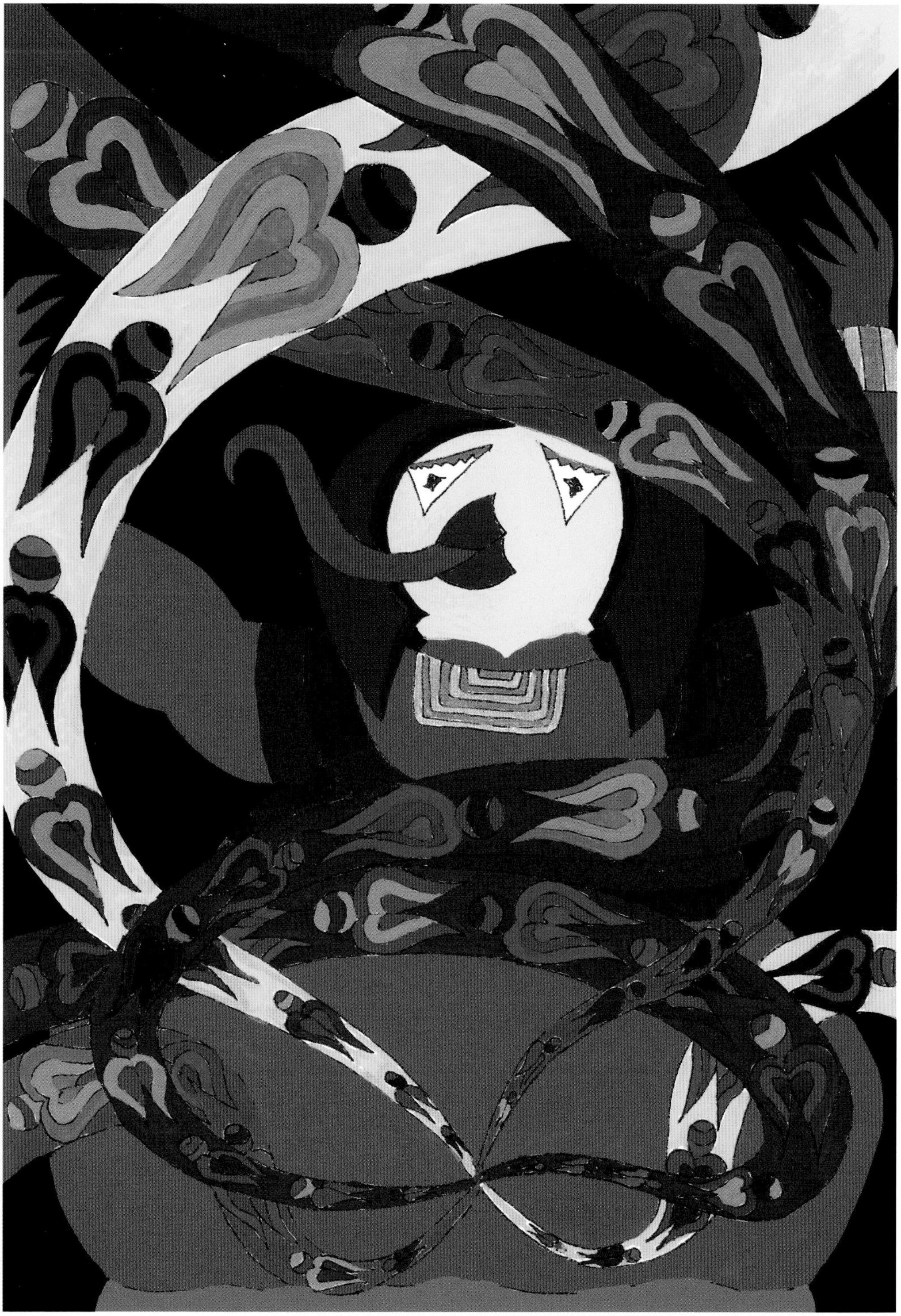

The sudden eruption of power and brightness caused a great explosion of blinding light. The explosion blasted off the roof of the cavern. It sent the castle tumbling down. The blinding light pulsated across the Land of Dreams.

The husks became once more Dreams of Destiny, full of life, colour and brightness longing to return to the persons from whom they had been stolen. As the Dreams of Destiny floated into the air shooting stars collected them and streaking across the sky, carried them back to the persons from whom they had been stolen.

As life, colour and, brightness spewed out of the belly of the Dream Thief a single claw extended from Snuggle's paw. It cut the net which bound him. Springing clear he freed the boys and Susan and prepared to protect them from attack.

But there was no need. For as life, colour and brightness returned to the Dreams of Destiny and the roof of the cavern exploded in bright pulsating light, the Dream Unicorn rose up. Restored to life it galloped through the sky, radiating power. It drew to itself the blackness and grey, turning all to glory.

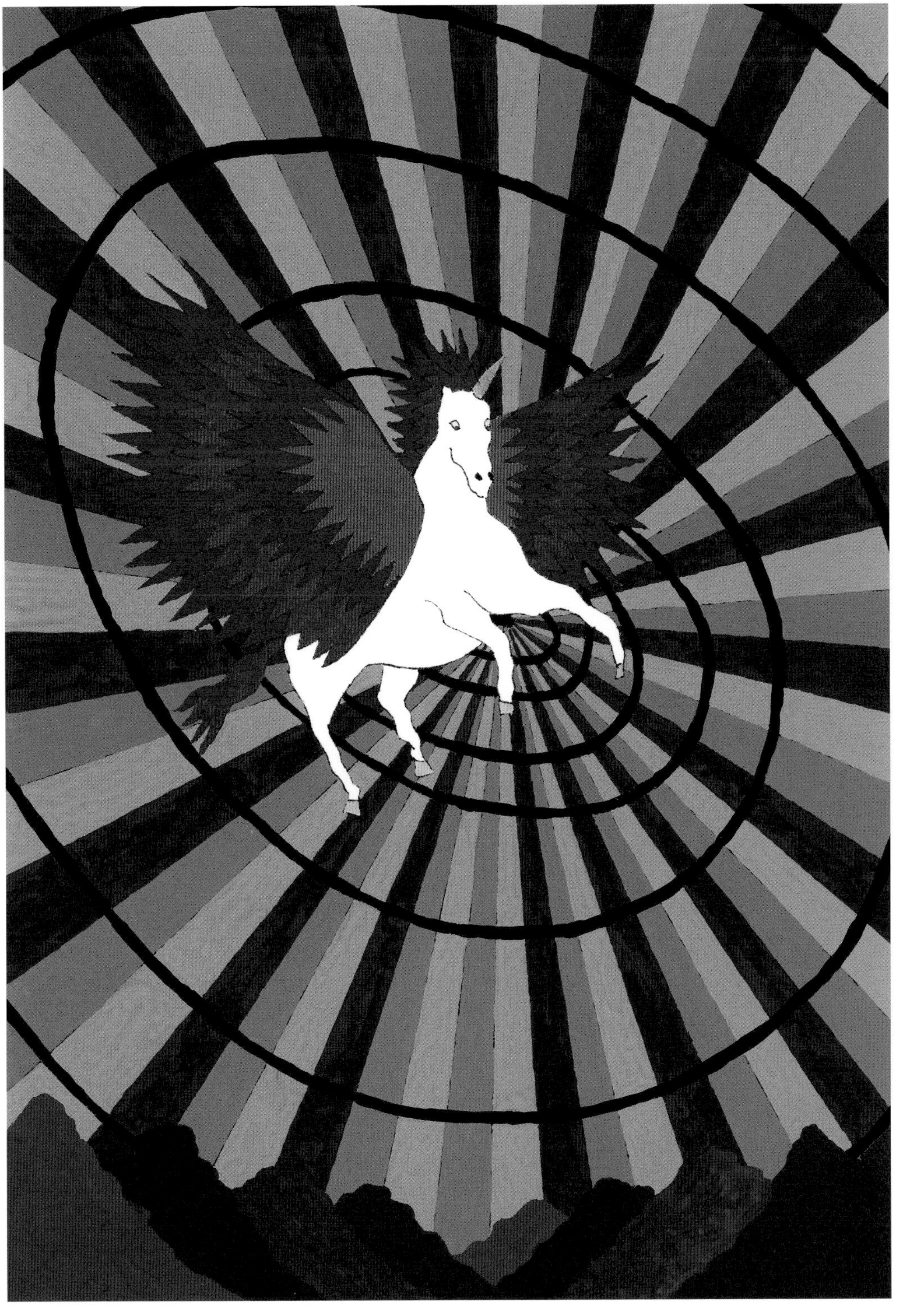

At the sight of the Dream Unicorn the Princess of the Night, her servants and the Dream Thief trembled and let out a great groan. They fled the Land of Dreams.

There were four Dreams of Destiny left in the remains of the cavern: the identical dreams of Alex and Susan (which were once more changing in myriad forms of different artistic creation), Little Dream and the secret dream which had followed Susan through the Land of Dreams: no one knew where she had come from.

Snuggle gathered up his powers as Dream Lord, declaimed words of magic and the identical dreams returned to Alex and Susan. Susan began to fade, to travel back through space and time to her home.

As Susan began to fade she called out to her sons, "Thank you for helping me get back my dream. And do not worry. I always wanted to be an artist. Now I know I want children as well!" for the secret dream had now become her dream: no one knew how.

"Thank goodness for that," sighed the brothers for throughout the adventure they had been nervous that once their mother saw what they were like and what trouble they got into she might decide not to have them.

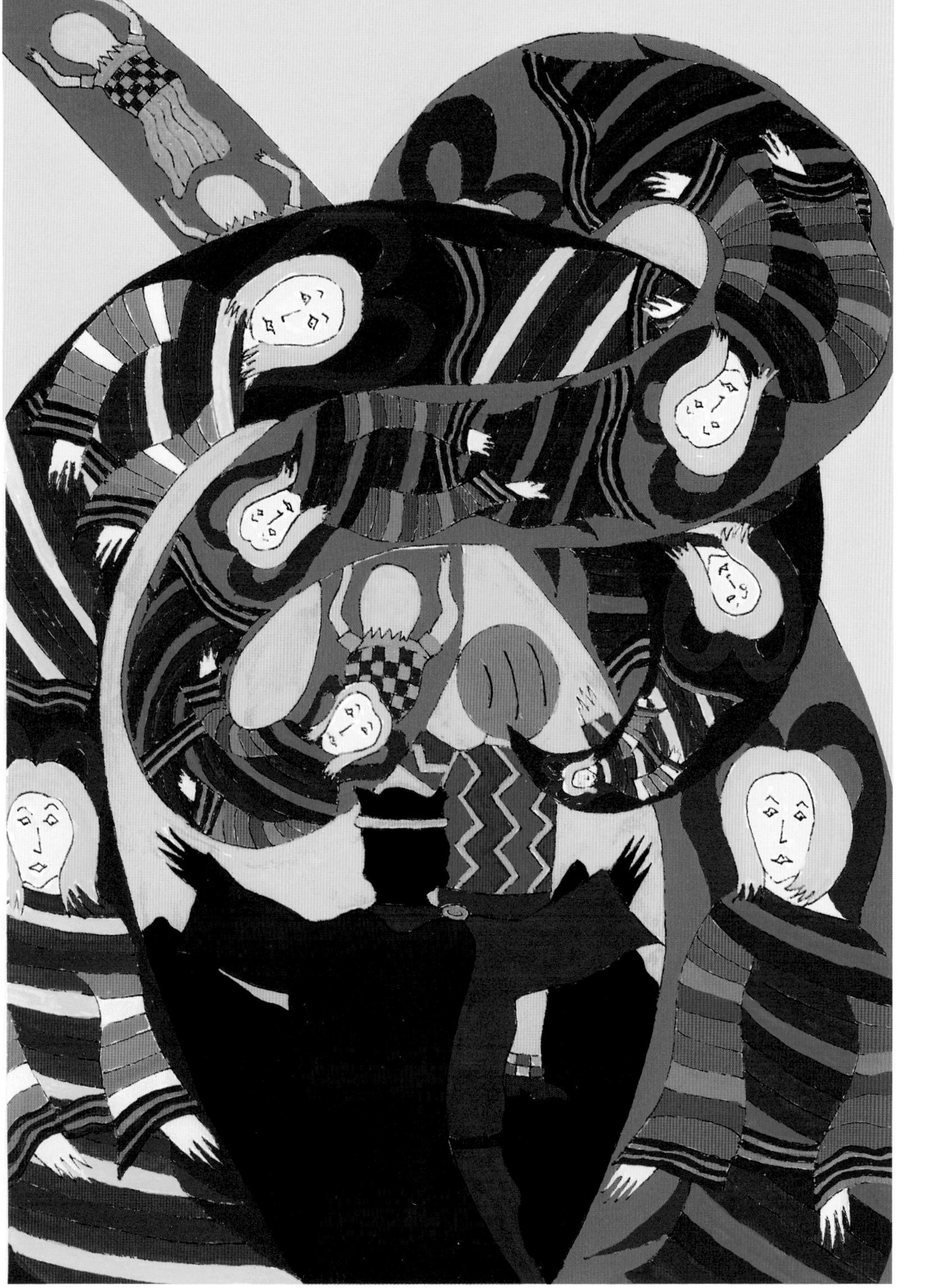

That left only Little Dream who was standing to one side. He felt that he could not say anything, but hoped he would not be forgotten.

"What about my dream?" asked Benjamin. "My brothers have got their dreams. I really want him."

"And I want Benjamin," added Little Dream.

Snuggle paused. He thought carefully before he replied. "I am a Dream Lord. I am a guardian of dreams. If you have a dream, I will fight to protect it. But I do not create dreams. It is not for me to decide who has what dream. That is above my calling. We shall go to the Gardener. He will decide what to do with Little Dream."

The cat breathed on the boys and Little Dream. They travelled through the void, landing on the hillside above the Garden where once more the Guide was there to greet them. They hurried down the gully to the door in the high brick wall which surrounded the Garden. It was still the Night of Dreams.

The Gardener stood beside the fire. Shooting stars streaked across the night sky. The Gardener was clearly pleased, but before he could say a word Benjamin blurted out, "I would like Little Dream. As my dream."

The Gardener did not reply, but simply lifted his arms and let out a sigh which rippled and danced through the Garden.

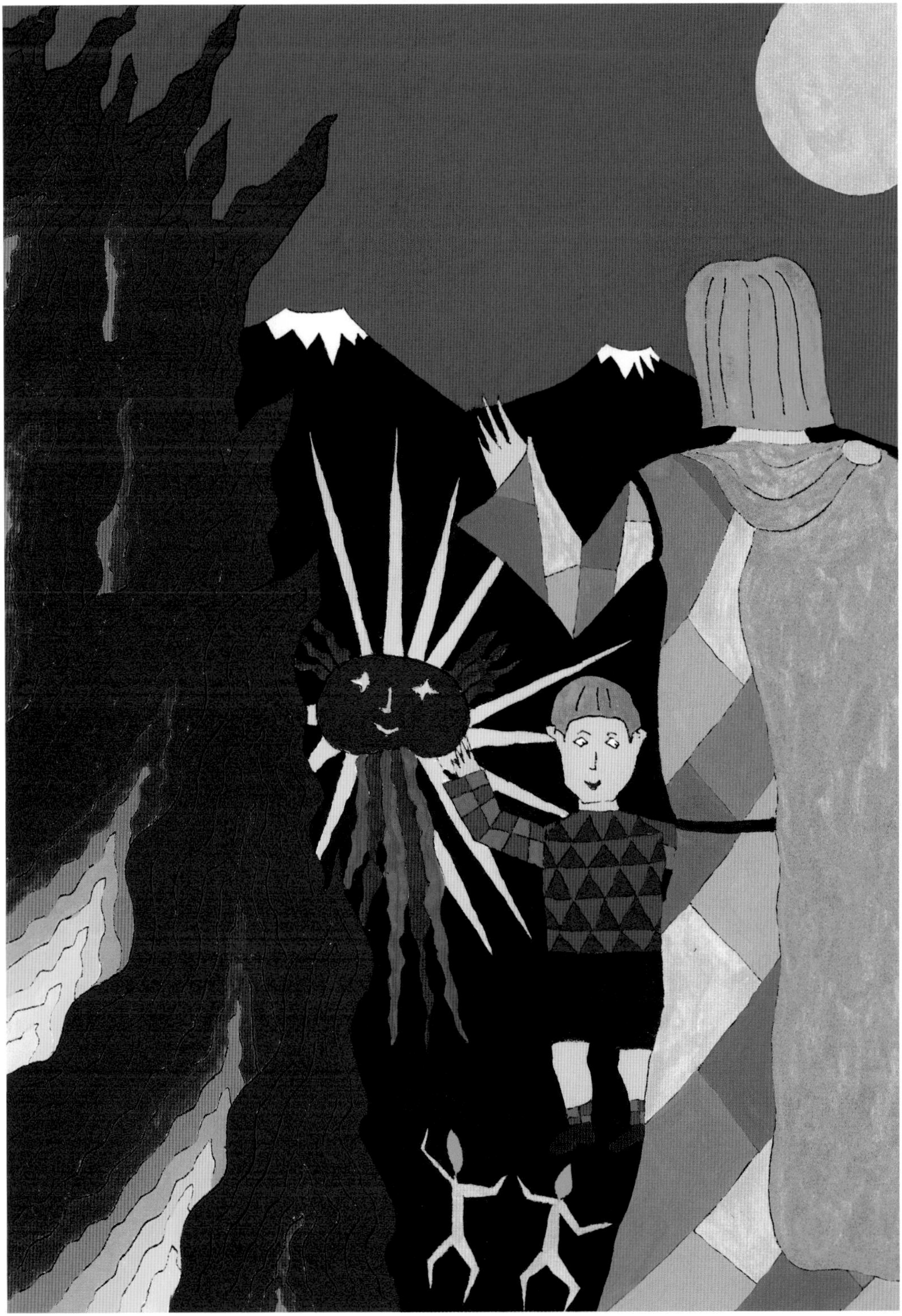

As the Gardener let out the sigh a shooting star shot through the sky, lifted up Little Dream and after arching high lodged the dream deep in Benjamin's breast. Benjamin smiled, and opening his mouth began to sing. The pure sound echoed through the Garden. "Wow!" cried his brothers, for they had never heard Benjamin sing before.

"What happened to Precious Dream Plant?" asked Julius. "Is she still in Little Dream?"

"No," the Gardener replied taking Precious Dream Plant out of his pocket. "Precious Plants live in the Garden, not in the breast of any mortal. Even though Benjamin does get into an awful lot of trouble and might have need of her."

So saying the Gardener led the boys and cat across the Garden to the fountain. The Guide played his flute and boys and cat danced through the waters emerging at the bottom of the garden of The Old Vicarage. The light was on in the studio. The boys looked up in the dark and saw their mother walk across the room paintbrush in her hand. She had started work on a new painting. She was happy.

"Mum's got back her dream!" the boys all cried. "Three cheers!" "Hip hip hooray!"

"And I've got Little Dream!" added Benje with a sigh.

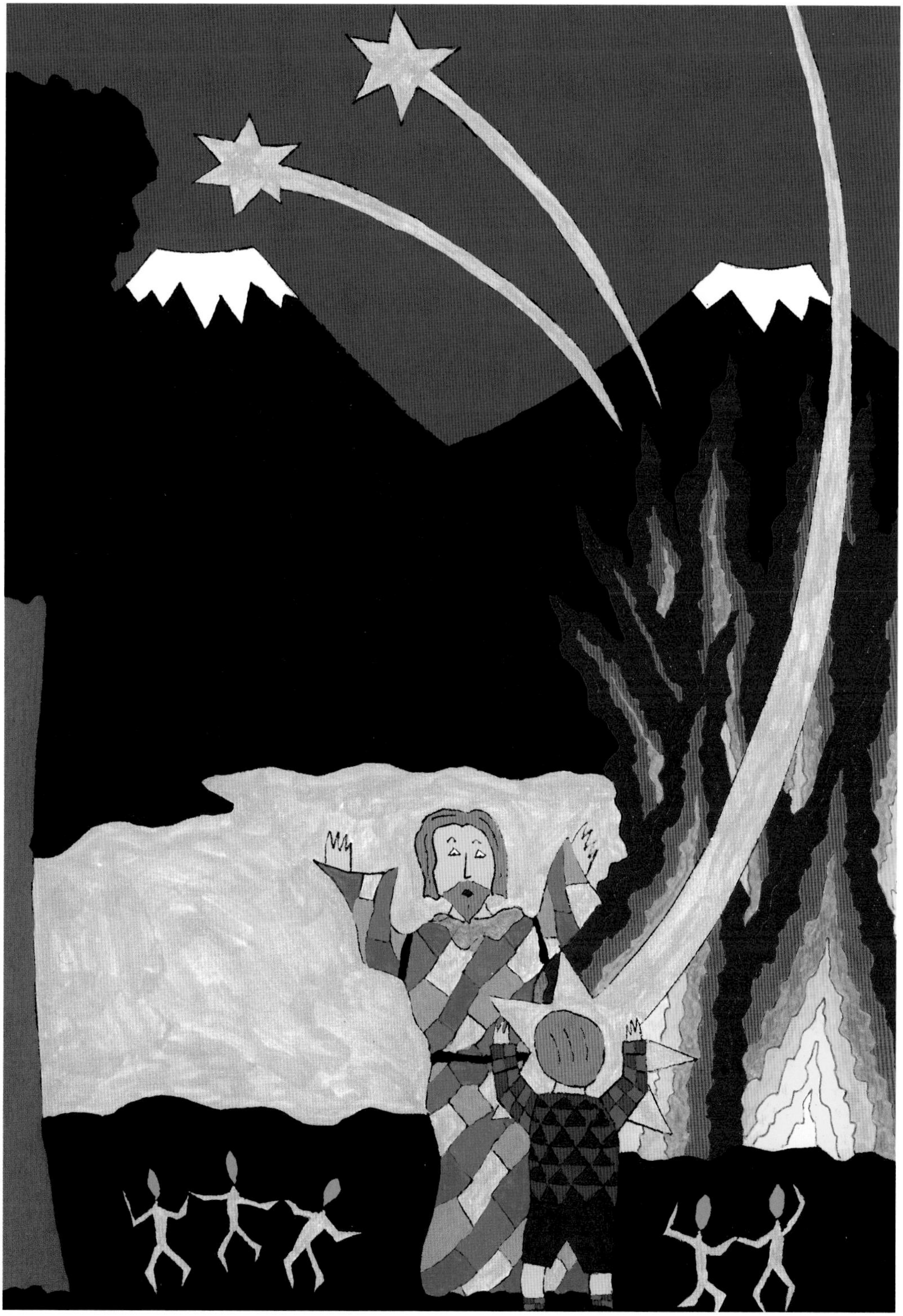

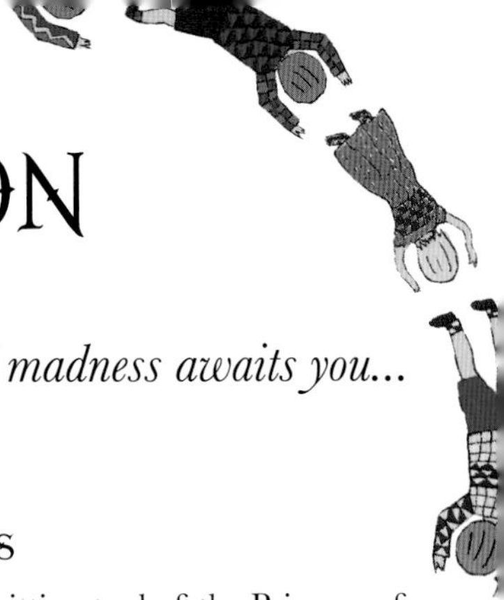

TALES OF RAMION

Blown away by The Dream Thief? More magic and madness awaits you...

Available Now:

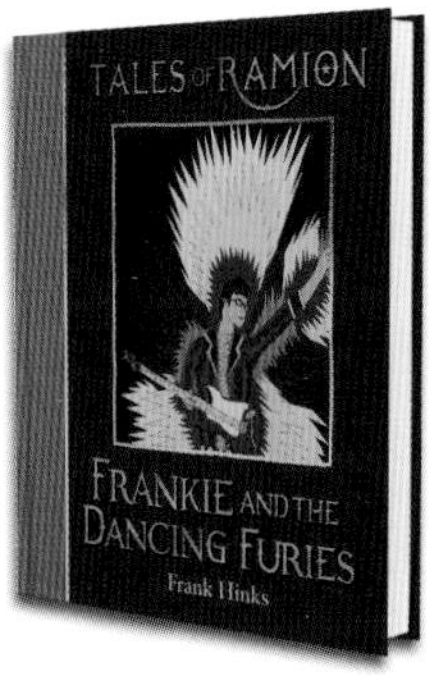

TALES OF RAMION
FRANKIE AND THE DANCING FURIES
Frank Hinks

FRANKIE AND THE DANCING FURIES

A storm summoned by the witch Griselda (unwitting tool of the Princess of the Night) attacks The Old Vicarage and carries off the boys' father along with Griselda, the skull Boris (whom the Princess wants for her living art collection), the dwarves and the boys' mother as a child. The father's love of rock and roll distorts the spell and all travel to the land of the Dancing Furies where the spirit of the great rock god Jimi (Hendrix) takes possession of the father's body. When he causes flowers to grow in the hair of the Dancing Furies they reveal their true nature as Goddesses of Vengeance.

ISBN: 9781909938083

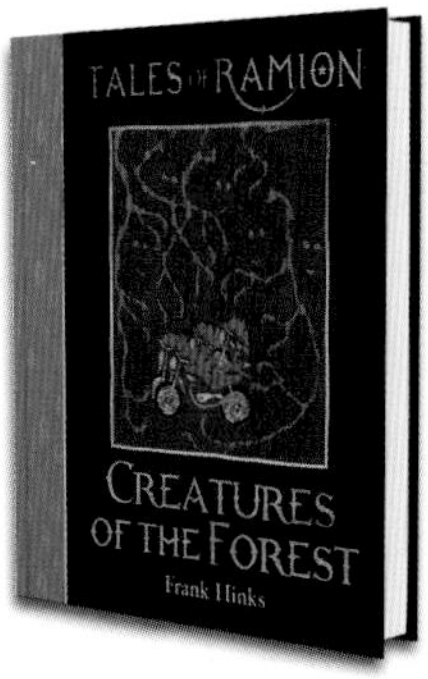

TALES OF RAMION
CREATURES OF THE FOREST
Frank Hinks

CREATURES OF THE FOREST

In the magical forest there are Globerous Ghosts, Venomous Vampires, Scary Scots and Mystic Mummies, who (like other mummies) cannot stand boys who pick their noses. The boys are in constant danger of being turned into ghostly globs, piles of dust or being exploded by very loud bagpipe music. Thankfully, Ducky Rocky, Racing Racoons and the Hero Hedgehogs are there to help.

ISBN: 9781909938144

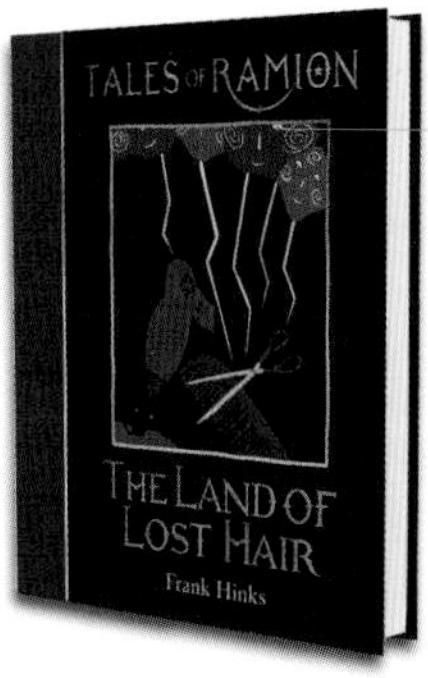

TALES OF RAMION
THE LAND OF LOST HAIR
Frank Hinks

THE LAND OF LOST HAIR

The witch Griselda casts a spell to make the boys travel to her, but the slime of maggot is past its sell-by date and the boys and their parents only lose their hair. Snuggle (Dream Lord and superhero) takes the boys to the Land of Lost Hair, but Griselda follows, and sends giant combs, scissors and hair driers to get the boys. "Boy kebabs for tea!" cried Griselda jubilantly.

ISBN: 9781909938106

And these deluxe collections that include three or four Tales

RAMION
Frank Hinks

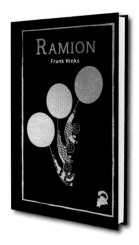

RAMION

ISBN: 9781909938038

ROCK OF RAMION
Frank Hinks

ROCK OF RAMION

ISBN: 9781909938045

SEAS OF RAMION
Frank Hinks

SEAS OF RAMION

ISBN: 9781909938014

You can explore the magical world of Ramion by visiting the website

www.ramion-books.com

Share Ramion Moments on Facebook

TALES of RAMION
FACT AND FANTASY

O nce upon a time not so long ago there lived in The Old Vicarage, Shoreham, Kent (a village south of London) three boys (Julius, Alexander and Benjamin) with their mother, father and Snuggle, the misnamed family cat who savaged dogs and had a weakness for the vicar's chickens. At birthdays there were magic shows with Scrooey-Looey, a glove puppet with great red mouth who was always rude.

The boys with Snuggle

J ulius was a demanding child. Each night he wanted a different story. But he would help his father. "Dad tonight I want a story about the witch Griselda" (who had purple hair like his artist mother) "and the rabbit Scrooey-Looey and it starts like this…" His father then had to take over the story not knowing where it was going (save that the witch was not allowed to eat the children). Out of such stories grew the Tales of Ramion which were enacted with the boys' mother as Griselda and the boys' friends as Griselda's guards, the Dim Daft Dwarves (a role which came naturally to children).

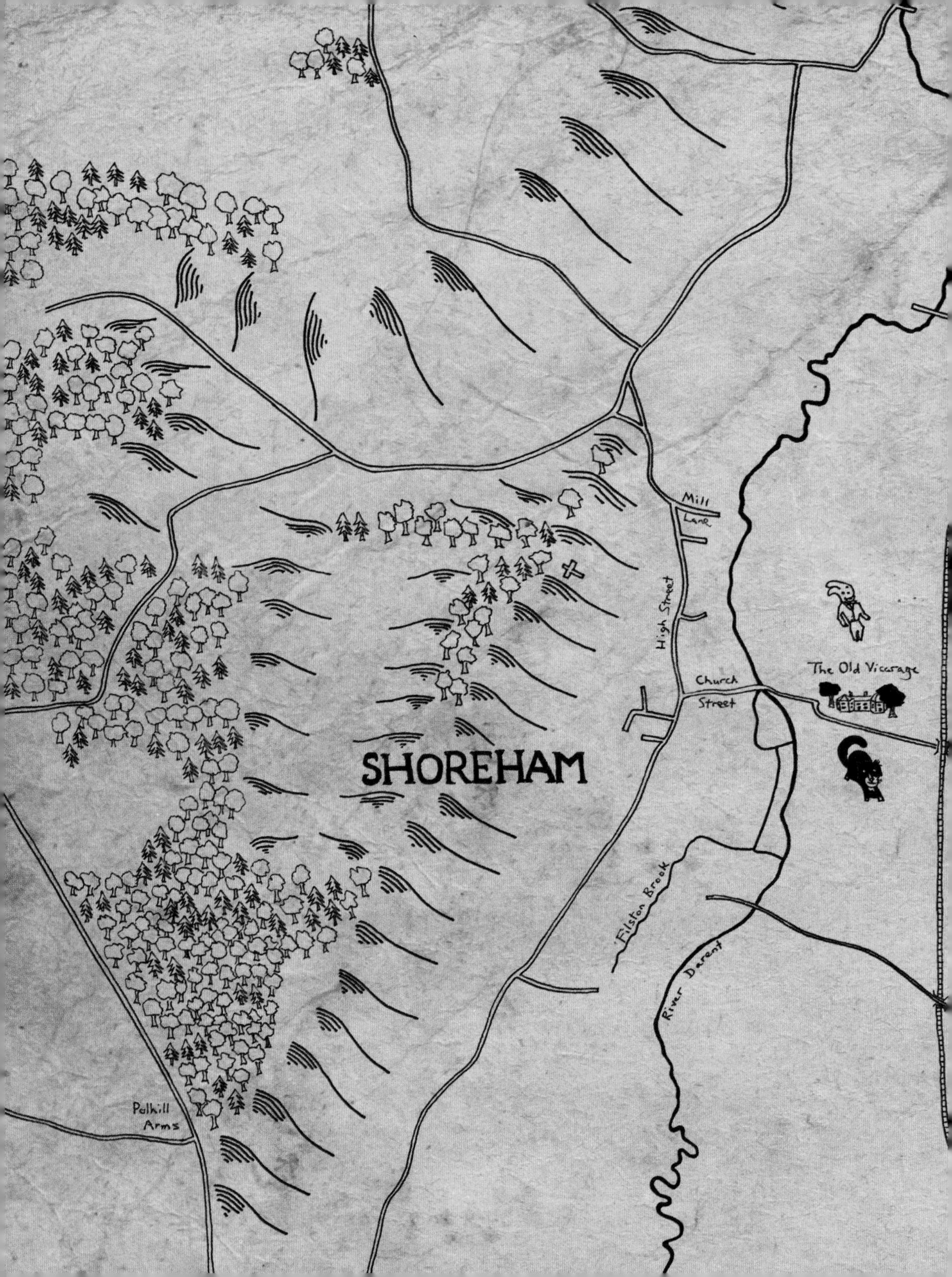

SHOREHAM
Mill Lane
High Street
Church Street
The Old Vicarage
Filston Brook
River Darent
Polhill Arms